FREAK NIGHTS

Acknowledgements

Some of these stories first appeared as follows: 'These Things Happen', 'There's Nothing Wrong With Me Now', 'A Nice Story' and 'Ciao, Bella' in 'New Irish Writing' in the *Irish Press;* 'Details' in *London Magazine;* 'The Lights of a Town in the Distance' in *London Magazine* and *The Second Blackstaff Book of Short Stories* (Blackstaff, 1991); 'Cities Beneath the Sea' in *Signals* (Constable, 1991); 'Of Course You Were' in 'New Irish Writing' in the *Sunday Tribune*; and 'Freak Nights' in the *Sunday Tribune*, the *Critical Quarterly* and *The Hennessy Book of Irish Fiction* (New Island Books, 1995). 'A Change in the Weather' won the 1987 RTÉ Francis MacManus Short Story Award, and later appeared in *Prize-Winning Radio Stories* (Mercier, 1994).

I would like to thank the following for their help and encouragement: Leo Cullen, Anthony Glavin, John McGahern, David Marcus and Alan Ross, as well as Liz, Angela and Jack.

Tá mé buíoch freisin de na daoine seo a leanas: An Bráthair de Barra, Seán Ó Leidhean, Justin Ó Morcháin; agus Aoife Ní Scolaí agus Seán Greally in Áras na nGael i nGaillimh, a chuir na scéalta seo ar dhiosca.

Above all, I would like to thank my father, Séamas, my sister, Mary (who typed most of the stories), and Fionnuala for their unfailing support.

CIARÁN FOLAN
FREAK NIGHTS
and Other Stories

Do Larry,

Tá súil agan go
mbeidh cúpla oíche
eile againn!

Cárán

**NEW
ISLAND
BOOKS**

FREAK NIGHTS
and Other Stories
is first published in 1996
in Ireland by
New Island Books,
2 Brookside,
Dundrum Road,
Dublin 14,
Ireland.

ISBN 1 874597 41 3

New Island Books receives financial assistance from
The Arts Council (An Chomhairle Ealaíon),
Dublin, Ireland.

Cover design by Jon Berkeley
Typeset by Graphic Resources
Printed in Ireland by Colour Books, Ltd.

In memory of my brother, Diarmaid

CONTENTS

A Nice Story

So, in July, the couple flew to Madrid, where they took a twin room in a small hotel near Puerta del Sol. They'd come to Spain to arrange things, but as it happened each had completely different sets of arrangements in mind. Such is often the case.

On the day of arrival they decided to walk around the old part of the city. After a while they found a nice bar, in the corner of Plaza Mayor, where they paid high prices for bottled beer and delicately designed sandwiches. But it was cheaper than Paris: they both agreed on this.

He complained about the heat. It was thirty degrees in the shade. She said, "What do you expect? It's a hot country."

They rubbed suntan lotion on each other's skin. They compared the colour of their faces, arms and legs. She won, she decided. When they returned to the hotel that evening they showered and changed their clothes.

All the while they talked a lot. She called it making conversation and it applied most especially in public places. So they conversed, to varying degrees, in cafés, restaurants, outside and inside the Prado, and on the metro. They talked too in the hotel room, but with more constraint.

It was late in the evening. They were at a café on the Gran Via. Let us call them the boy and the girl for, though they were both somewhat older than those words suggest, it suits the purposes of the story.

She, the blonde girl of slight build, was wearing a white blouse, a loose-fitting black skirt and low-heeled black sandals. She also had a pair of diamante earrings on. He, dark-haired and thin, was wearing a white shirt, light grey trousers and espadrilles. By this stage they both looked quite tanned.

They sat at a table near the doorway, together, so that they faced the street and could watch the people passing by. This is true.

They'd been talking about matters in their own country, which was depressing, so they talked about smoking instead. (She did, he didn't). They'd discussed all this on many occasions in varied locations before. When that topic was finished with (she was, he wasn't), there came a pause in the conversation. They each drank more beer.

Then he said, "I want to sleep with you."

This was something she'd heard before, so, of course, she wasn't surprised at all.

"Oh, come on," she said and laughed.

"Exactly," he said, but he was serious.

She stared out at the traffic sweeping along the Gran Via and sighed. She was absent-mindedly tearing a beer mat into tiny pieces and letting them drop into a small pile in front of her. It was a habit he had only begun to notice since they had come away on holidays together.

"I thought we'd been through all this before," she said and lit a cigarette.

"We could go though it again," he said, watching the smoke from her cigarette drifting up into the hot Spanish air.

While they were talking, an argument had broken out at a nearby table between a group of prostitutes and a man who had apparently been drinking with them all evening. Two waiters had grabbed the man and pushed him out onto the street. Now he stood on the pavement, shouting abuse at the women.

"Look at him," the girl said. "What kind of life do you think he has? Can you imagine his wife and children?"

The boy glanced at the drunken man. "Who cares?" he said.

"Answer me this," the girl said. "Could you ever see yourself ending up like that?"

He studied the man for a moment. His hair looked greasy and unwashed; his beige suit was worn and stained. There was a pink carnation stuck in his lapel.

"Anything is possible," the boy said.

"But could you? Ever?"

"I don't know," he said. "Perhaps. Maybe."

She lit another cigarette and stared out once more at the traffic, her earrings catching the last of the evening light. Around them, Madrid was slipping into darkness; the avenues and streets were filling with voices.

They were in the hotel room. The girl was having a shower. The boy stood by the open window. People moved slowly through the narrow street below. A crowd had gathered around a man doing a three-card trick. Everyone seemed to be winning but the man was grinning and his partner was shouting, all the more to attract the punters.

Was she playing a trick to keep him at bay? He wondered how a thing like this could happen. How could he have missed the point so much? Was she fooling him all along or had he been fooling himself?

The girl got dressed. She brushed her hair. The boy watched her from the window. He knew the story but he still felt a strong desire for her. He knew this was foolish and without point. He really wanted to be alone.

Between drinks and conversations they visited historic and beautiful locations. They took a day trip to Segovia and one to El Escorial. They watched an open-air theatrical spectacle with fireworks. They searched for a night club that played the right music, but they failed to find one. Occasionally they read late into the night. She read *Tender is the Night*, while he read *Remembrance of Things Past*. All of this is quite true.

In the afternoons they went frequently to the Retiro, a large public park with a lake, on the edge of the city. She wanted to hire a boat, he wouldn't. It was on one of these visits to the Retiro that another talk took place.

They chose a table in the shade of a large tree, some distance from a small ramshackle bar. He ordered a mineral water *con gaz*, but she had a beer. There had been a lot of silences between them for most of the day.

He was watching a pale yellow airship which had just floated into view—carrying an advertisement for ice-cream, as far as he could make out—when she finally started talking.

"Isn't it amazing how life can be so simple for ages, and then you wake up one morning and it's just so fucking complicated. I don't suppose that's ever happened to you, has it?"

She had taken off her sunglasses. There was a faint line of perspiration along her upper lip and the skin beneath her eyes was dark. She hadn't been sleeping well; it was obvious to him now.

"Listen," she said, "there's something I should have told you before we came out here, but for some reason I thought it would be easier away from home."

It was complicated, she said. She didn't know how she could explain it easily. She had a very important and very difficult decision to make. And, suddenly, she was talking about this other person and something he had asked her.

"I hope you're going to try to understand," she said. "I don't want you getting up on your high horse about this."

"Isn't this fun," he said.

She ignored the comment. She looked at him across the table. This time they were in a restaurant, eating paella.

He'd told her about paella a long time ago, but this was the first time they'd had it. There was a lot of rice, and very little else. The girl had ordered a bottle of wine.

She said, "At least we might as well have something right to drink." He said he didn't want any. She drank it herself.

"You're really great crack," she said.

"I know," he said.

"You're making me feel miserable," she said.

He kept on eating.

"You've no grace," she said. "That's what's wrong with you, you know."

Finally she stubbed out her cigarette. "This is where it ends, I suppose," she said, and got up to go. She left enough money to cover her half of the bill. He didn't say a thing.

This is where it ends, in a way. The girl went back to the hotel room and stayed that night. As she was packing next morning the boy was still in bed, but she knew he was awake, watching her. When she was leaving she said "Goodbye" and he said "Goodbye," without raising his head. She got the next plane home. Months later he heard that she'd got married. This was what he had expected.

The boy stayed on in Madrid for another week. He spent a lot of time now in the bars in the poorer part of the city. He drank too much and tried making conversation with the girls who lingered, idly and languidly, in these places. But he didn't fall into bad company; he felt too sorry for himself, and told himself he really wasn't interested.

Cities Beneath the Sea

The summer of the year I am to be sent away to boarding school. My mother switches on the television on a particular afternoon and a dimly lit landscape fills the corner of the room. The secrets of the moon pour into our lives. My mother says a boundary has been crossed. She says now there are no limits beyond which Man cannot go. My father lights a cigarette. He pokes it at the screen. He says, "Anything the Yanks do, the Communists can't be far behind." My mother gazes at the screen—the slow-bouncing shadow of Neil Armstrong reflected in her eyes.

For years my mother has made predictions—the end of wars, cities beneath the sea, a universal language, pills for food, a bridge across the Atlantic, a man on Mars. Some of these are already coming to pass before our very eyes she says. And who can doubt her. My father reads somewhere that it is all a million-dollar NASA stunt. Everything was set up in a studio in the desert. They never even left the ground he tells my mother.

"Oh Tom," she says, "why do they print such nonsense?"

She looks out at the sky and, for a moment, a faint doubt floats across her mind.

Australia is my father's country, it seems. He talks about the bush and the territories, the great open spaces and the outback with an ease suggesting familiarity. During the winter, he says they're scorching now on Bondi Beach. He checks the temperatures in the paper every day. He talks about the flowers of the jacaranda tree.

"Petals like the tears of a goddess," he says.

My mother laughs. Sometimes she says, "Your father's Australia is a state of mind."

My mother has work to do. She runs the village post office. In the evenings and during the holidays she gets me to help. I count change, stamp letters, sort postal orders and deal with customers when she's tired. My father takes no part in the business.

"Your father has no head for figures," my mother says by way of explanation.

Instead, my father travels around to old farmhouses and buys antiques. That's what he calls them when he's discussing them with my mother, but with the farmers they are "knick-knacks" and "stuff lying about". Mainly we visit the houses of bachelors. These houses are always up high-hedged winding lanes. They have apple trees and gooseberry bushes at the back or side. I wander around kicking windfalls while my father sits in the kitchen drinking whiskey and discussing football. Sometimes one of these men plays a tune on the fiddle. My father winks at me as I stand in the doorway.

Driving away, he tells me to have a look at what's in the box on the back seat.

"Take them out," he says. "Take them out for God's sake."

I pull out a blue glazed jug, a large brown willow-pattern dinner plate, an olive-shaded oil lamp, sun-bleached linen tablecloths from a long-forgotten wedding party.

"Some bloody caper," my father shouts. He opens the window and starts to whistle. The tune is always 'Waltzing Matilda' and I always try to sing the loudest.

Every so often the car is packed with cardboard boxes full of crockery and lamps and we all take off for Dublin. We stay, three to a room, in a hotel and next day we do the rounds of the antique shops on the quays. My mother always does the dealing. Before she enters a shop she studies herself in her compact mirror. Then she looks at my father and raises an eyebrow and smiles and he gives a low clear whistle. We wait on the footpath, sitting on heavy brown sofas that bear signs reading 'Do Not Touch'. My father lights a cigarette and I eat ice-cream and we listen for the sounds of money changing hands. If we manage to sell everything in a day they argue about whether we should stay another night. "Money is there to be spent," my mother says and she reaches back to squeeze my knee. She says, "Life is short" and "You can't take it with you when you go."

"Yes," says my father. "This caper will surely land us in the poorhouse yet."

Thunderclouds bank up behind the line of beeches at the end of the garden. My mother tries on another sunhat.

"So, what do you think?" She stands with one hand on her hip.

My father looks up from the table. He jots something in his note book. "*Bellissima*," he says. He is looking at my mother as if he can't remember exactly who she is.

"Indeed," my mother says. She picks up another hat, then heedlessly drops it back in the box. "The sun," she says, "has deserted us forever."

She goes to the window. Whenever she does this she stands on the tips of her toes. But the window is large and my mother is not small. She is like a child looking at a world she has heard mention of in passing.

As his first great undertaking of the summer my father plans to build a telescope. He gets measurements from a magazine. He makes a list of materials. One Saturday he brings a length of six-inch-diameter plastic piping home from town. He writes away to England for further information. He orders lenses. I study maps of the sky.

Three weeks later a wooden crate packed with straw arrives by special delivery. As my father lifts a lens from the crate it crashes to the floor.

"Australia here we come," my mother says. My father doesn't move. My mother gets a brush and starts to sweep up.

Ever since her sister Jean brought word of it home from Chicago, my mother's summer drink is iced tea.

"Everything stops for iced tea," my father says. He holds a jug in front of his face before pouring the clouded liquid down the sink.

My mother, in her sunhat, is sitting on a café terrace somewhere in a hot country. She idly tips her glass towards a dallying stranger. The hour is full of tinkling and a thousand shifting points of glass-refracted light.

One Friday afternoon my mother puts me in charge of the post office and goes to town. Near closing time an old man comes in. He stands in the middle of the floor and peers about. When he spots me he takes off his hat and shakes it in my direction.

"I want to speak to somebody in charge," he says.

"I am," I say.

"Not you," he says. "I want to speak to your mother. Where is she? I have questions to ask her."

I tell him she's gone to town.

"Ask her whose money she's spending," he says as he leaves. "Just ask her that, sonny boy."

After he's gone the room echoes with the smell of drink and damp turf fires.

That evening, as she waltzes about the kitchen in a new pair of white sandals, stocking up the fridge with fruit and bottles of soda water, I tell my mother about the customers.

"Nobody cranky, I hope, she says.

"No," I say and she smiles and hands me a cool peach.

My mother locks the sitting-room door. The voice of John McCormack escapes into the quivering afternoon. A boy, wheeling a bike, stops on the road for a moment. He looks at the sky and then at the vacant windows of our house.

My father produces a typewriter. He keeps it in the garage where our car used to be. My mother makes mugs of percolated coffee in the morning and glasses of lemonade as the day gets warm, and leaves them outside the garage door. She says he is writing a novel. She says this with pride and conviction. My father never mentions it at all. On his breaks from work he stands at the garage door in his trousers and vest. He pushes his hand through his hair and lights another cigarette. He looks like the writers I have seen in photographs in his old magazines—intense men with two-day shadows staring at some invisible point on a black-and-white horizon. "What a caper," he says to himself as he stubs out a half-smoked cigarette.

My mother takes to preparing extravagant meals. "A writer's brain needs nourishment," she says. She studies numerous cookbooks. She carefully notes the ingredients, the quantities and times. But somewhere along the line she loses patience with all the instructions and goes at it in her own way. She smiles at my father as she puts a new dish on the table. She watches him eat and waits for his approval. "*Buonisimo*," he always says. He must wonder though how long his luck will hold.

On a hot afternoon in late August a man calls to the post office. He is dressed in a suit and tie, and carrying a briefcase. He tells me to fetch my mother. ("Fetch" is the word he uses.) She is sitting on the sofa in the front room, drinking iced tea, leafing through a magazine.

"Oh love," she whispers. "A man in a suit on a day like this." She fingers the neck of her blouse as she watches him through the crack at the jamb of the door.

The man and my mother go into the front room. He puts his hands on the briefcase and starts to speak. My mother nods. She arranges her skirt. He takes some papers from the briefcase and hands them to my mother. She spreads them on the coffee table beside her. She glances quickly from one paper to the other and then at the man. He checks his watch and says something again. A breeze, a fickle movement of air, lifts one of the papers off the table. My mother reaches out to grasp it and knocks against a jug full of poppies. She picks up a flower and holds it to her face. The man stares at the red explosion on the carpet. Then he checks his watch again.

"Neither of us were much good at figures, as it turns out," my mother says.

She runs a finger along the edge of the counter, checking for dust. Already everything has been scrubbed and cleared.

"Someday," she says, "you will remember all this and you'll want to ask questions. Listen, don't think back. Don't stop in your life just to wonder about this. Don't fill up your life with dreams of things that may be or that might have been. You mustn't be like your father and myself."

She tears a page from the calendar block and now it is a new day. In the yard my father carries boxes of magazines from the garage and flings them on to the fire. It flares blue and red for a few seconds before burning with a low grey flame.

"That awful smell," my mother says eventually, "will get into everything."

I remember this now though it never happened. My mother and father are walking through the fields, which are not their fields anymore. I am somewhere else. Perhaps I don't exist. My father is carrying a guitar slung over his shoulder. My mother is wearing a pale green sunhat and a blue dress with a large white flower. She is barefoot. Now she notices a moon, hanging low like a fragment of shattered crystal in the late evening sky. It reminds her of something. She turns to my father.

"We are thieves and petty criminals," she shouts.

"Yes," shouts my father, "we are that."

He unslings his guitar and starts to strum, but it is out of tune. My mother spins around once, then sashays across the field.

"Play," she shouts, "play anyway."

Jangle, jangle, jangle the guitar goes. Jangle, jangle.

My father starts to laugh. Next he's singing. Some song he wrote during all the idle garage days. My mother keeps moving far, far away, until she can no longer hear my father's voice, until she can hear only those jangling notes that sound to her like the strange radio signals emitted by the unmanned stars.

There's Nothing Wrong With Me Now

The first thing to do was to clear away the toys. He threw the large plastic building bricks into a cardboard box, put Bosco on top, and stuck the box into a corner of the press beside the fireplace. Then he noticed the small, white teddy bear lying face-down under the table. He hid the teddy behind a cushion on the couch.

Next he took the cloth off the table and brought in glasses from the kitchen. He carried in the bottle of Bushmills and the soda water, and the beer and arranged these on the table beside the glasses.

He opened a can of Heineken and drank some. He looked at his watch, then went upstairs to the bedroom. The baby was asleep.

Just after nine o'clock, the doorbell rang. It was Dave.

"Hard night on the roads tonight, Mick," said Dave, stepping into the hallway. He threw his coat and scarf on the couch and then stood in front of the fireplace, rubbing his hands. "It's bloody freezing."

Mick poured some whiskey and handed it to Dave. "Get that into you," he said.

Dave took a quick gulp of the whiskey. "Jesus," he said, "I've three sets of papers still to correct and the results are going out on Friday."

"I've one left," said Mick. "Second-year Maths."

"To hell with it," said Dave, pouring himself another whiskey.

They had started into the beer when Tony arrived.

"Hi," said Tony, looking around. "Is this the party? Is this it?"

"Looks like it," said Dave. "The party starts now."

Tony took a can and a glass from the table. He said, "Plenty of booze, anyway, and plenty of time to get rid of it. And no women to annoy us."

"At least not any wives to annoy us," said Dave.

"Excuse me, Dave."

"Doesn't worry me," said Dave. "Not yet." He grinned.

"Ya boy," said Tony. "Just wait a few years. Then you'll see what it's all about." He looked at Mick. "Isn't that right?"

Mick said nothing.

Tony put his empty glass down on the table. "God, it's very quiet," he said. "How about some music?" He went over to the stereo and looked through the records and tapes. He picked out four LPs. "It's okay to put something on, isn't it?" he asked, turning to Mick.

Mick said, "Just keep the volume down a bit."

"No problem," said Tony, putting on the first side of Elvis Costello's 'Trust'. "Listen to this," he said. "Haven't heard this in years."

He sat back down at the table. "Any cards?" he asked.

"I don't think so," said Mick. "They went missing after the last time."

"Doesn't matter," said Tony. "Anyway, I'd hate to leave ye all broke again."

All three sat at the table. They drank beer, and every so often Mick would pour each of them a whiskey. They talked.

Elvis Costello was singing 'Shot With His Own Gun'.

Tony had been talking.

"Jesus," he said, "wives can be an awful scourge."

Nobody else said anything.

"They can," Tony said again. "Take my wife, for example. Take her."

"No thanks," said Dave.

"No, seriously," said Tony. He poured the last of the whiskey. "I'm deadly serious."

"I believe you," said Dave. "I do."

Tony continued. "Or take your wife," he said, looking at Mick.

"What about her?" Mick said.

Tony ignored the question. "The difference is," he said, turning to Dave, "the difference is this man's wife is something special. Wouldn't you agree?"

Dave started to laugh. "Whatever you say, Tony," he said.

Tony held his empty glass up to the light, turning it slowly in his hand, watching the light shine through it. "She just radiates a certain something, if you know what I mean."

"I don't know what you're on about," said Dave, reaching for another can of Heineken.

"Of course you don't," said Tony, holding out his hand, waiting for Dave to pass him a fresh can.

"Is someone going to tell me what all this is about?" said Mick.

Tony looked at him; he was grinning. "Ask Dave, the expert. He'll tell you." He stood up. "I'm bursting. I'm going up to the jakes."

When Tony had left the room, Mick said, "What the fuck was that all about?"

"Nothing," said Dave. "You know you shouldn't pass any remarks on Tony, especially when he has a few drinks on him."

"So, why are you getting all defensive about it?"

"Listen, Mick. I don't know what Tony is on about and I certainly have no idea what you're on about. So, why don't we just drop it?"

"What did he mean: 'Ask Dave, the expert'?"

"He's a bit pissed, can't you see. None of us are exactly sober. He's talking shit. Tony's talking shit. What's new?"

"It didn't sound like shit to me."

"I give up," said Dave. He went over to the stereo and picked up an album called 'Ella Sings the Rodgers & Hart Songbook'. He was reading down the list of tracks when Tony came back in.

"Silence is golden," said Tony, shaking some of the opened cans that were scattered about the table. When he found one that wasn't empty, he sat back in his chair. "Well," he said, "that baby upstairs is very quiet. Not a squeak out of the creature. Did you notice that, Dave?"

"No," said Dave, "I didn't."

"Good man, Dave," said Tony. "Whatever you say, say nothing."

"Leave the baby out of this," said Mick.

"Jeez," said Tony, "I was only asking."

"Leave it," Mick said again.

"Leave it, Tony," said Dave. "OK?"

"Okay," said Tony. He took a long drink from his can. "Sorry I was born."

The orchestra began to play, and Ella Fitzgerald started to sing 'The Lady is a Tramp'.

After a while, Tony asked, "Where is she, anyway?"

"What the fuck's wrong with you tonight?" said Mick.

Tony looked at him. "I was just wondering, that's all."

"Well, if you really want to know: she, as you call her, my wife, is at work right now, at the restaurant, to be precise."

Tony looked at his watch. "At ten past one?" he asked.

Mick checked his own watch. "Well, then she'll be at Marie's place. That's the usual. Now, any more questions?"

"I don't think so," said Tony.

They were silent for a few moments. Then, Mick stood up. "I'm going to make a phone call," he said. "Is it OK with everyone if I ring my wife?"

"Of course, it's OK," said Dave. "Go on. Ring away."

Mick looked at Tony. "Is it all right with you?"

Tony was tapping his beer can against the edge of the table. He nodded.

Mick went out to the hall. He picked up the receiver, then put it down.

He picked it up again and dialled Marie's number. He held the receiver to his ear and heard the quick clicking sound, and then the number ringing out at the other end. He waited. It kept ringing.

He looked at his watch and started to count. He'd counted to forty-five when the line went dead. He replaced the receiver and waited a few minutes. He could hear the music, and Dave talking, inside.

He went back in and sat on the arm of the couch. Dave handed him a can of beer. "Everything okay?" he asked.

"Yeah," Mick said. "She's with Marie. She's staying another while and then she's coming home. She sends her regards."

"That's great," said Dave.

"Wonderful," said Tony.

At a quarter-past-two, Dave said, "Well, I'm off. I have to face the sixth-years in the morning."

Tony said, "Don't worry about them."

"Easy knowing you never had to stand in front of a class with a sore head on you," said Dave. "I wouldn't wish it on my worst enemy. Come on, I'll leave you home."

"No," Tony said, "I can manage."

"Better not chance it."

Tony stood up. "OK," he said. "Maybe I shouldn't, after all."

Dave went out and sat into his car. He started the engine and let it run. He got out again and began to spray de-icer on the windscreen.

Tony and Mick waited at the hall door. Tony said, "You know, anything I said tonight, forget it. Just forget it."

Then he hurried out to Dave's car. He was about to get in, when he looked back at Mick and shouted, "Sure, if we can't have an oul slag we might as well be fucking dead."

As the car pulled out, Dave beeped the horn and waved. Mick stood at the open door for a minute. The road was quiet. There were no lights to be seen in any of the houses across the way. Tony's second-hand Alfa Romeo lay glistening and silent beneath its covering of frost. He looked up at the sky. It was full of stars. He could see the Plough, Orion. Cygnus and Cepheus. Cassiopeia. Others, whose names he had forgotten.

He went back into the house. Ella Fitzgerald was singing in the living-room. The song about Manhattan. He turned off the stereo, shut the living-room door and went upstairs.

In the bedroom, the baby was asleep. In the light from the landing he examined carefully the baby's face and the shape of its nose and ears. He did this for a long time.

Then, he pulled the blanket down off the sleeping baby and looked at its small body, curled up. Carefully, he lifted it out of the cot. He held it in his left arm and put the fingers of his right hand to the baby's throat. The skin was soft and warm. The baby moved its head and made a sound, a sound like gurgling, and put a tightly closed fist up to its mouth.

A car passed on the road outside. He heard the clock ticking in the hall below. Another car passed, then slowed and stopped a short distance up the road.

He put the baby back in the cot and went to the window. The road was silent and empty.

He pulled the curtains closed and sat down on the bed. The baby was breathing softly now. He waited.

He was beginning to fall asleep when he heard the hall door being opened. He heard her in the hallway and then, more cautiously, on the stairs and on the landing. She turned on the light and stared at him sitting there on the edge of the bed. Her eyes were as bright as stars.

She said nothing, but rushed over to the cot. The baby was still asleep. Gently, she tucked the bedclothes up under the baby's chin.

Then, she looked at her husband again.

She said, "Is something the matter? Is it? Answer me."

"No," he said. "No. I'm all right now. There's nothing wrong with me now."

He looked at his wife standing there, her hands resting on the side of the cot. He could just barely make out the shapes of her body beneath her overcoat. He could hear nothing but the ticking of the clock and the baby's breathing.

The Lights Of A Town In The Distance

"I'm fed up telling everyone the bad in this relationship" is what Cathy says at some unearthly hour of the morning. She'd been talking about her life with Alan. She'd made no mention of anything very disturbing before this. There were none of the terrible revelations I've come to expect when people begin to open up, in that way that they invariably do, in the small hours. But we'd been drinking and I suppose she believed she was saying something of interest. Or perhaps I just wasn't paying attention. I spent the time looking at her face and neck, imagining the whiteness of the rest of her body. And her sister Emer sat there, silent, and I wondered if she could realise what was going on.

It turns out that Cathy firmly believes Alan has been seeing another woman. He's been making a lot of trips to Dublin all through the winter months. Business trips of sorts. Cathy has no proof, but she has a feeling. "And you know Cathy's feelings," says Emer.

I met Alan once, a year or so ago, in the departure lounge of Dublin airport, when Cathy and himself were flying out for some kind of lovers' weekend in London. He was wearing a faded denim jacket and jeans and he had an earring in one ear. And although we did little more than exchange pleasantries after Cathy's bright-eyed introduction, it struck me that he was already elsewhere, working out an escape route to another life, perhaps.

"I don't know when we're going to see an end to Cathy's unhappiness," Emer says. This is how she usually brings up some story concerning Cathy and her life with men. There are many such stories.

Once, Cathy met a man while she was working in an Italian restaurant off Grafton Street. "She must have known him for exactly the amount of time it takes to order a pizza and a cup of coffee." Next thing Cathy was in London, ringing Emer, begging her to wire over one hundred pounds. That was in 1974, when Cathy was seventeen and a hundred pounds meant something. Emer managed to gather some money together to get herself over on the boat. She found Cathy in a place in Kentish Town. "There she was in this kip with this sleaze-ball Arab." It turned out to be a false alarm. Cathy wasn't pregnant like Emer thought she was, and after a week of seeing the sights they both returned to Dublin.

Ten years ago Cathy took up with an acrobat. They toured the country in his brightly coloured caravan. Late one night, after he'd been drinking, he held a knife to her throat and forced her up onto the ladder leading to the tightrope. He told her he was God and that he could fly. Then he told her what he'd been trying to tell her for months. That he was leaving this shit-hole country and going back to his wife and kids in Marseilles. "Thirty feet above the ground, with a knife at your throat, is no place for feeling broken-hearted."

In her late twenties Cathy fell for an estate agent she met in a Leeson Street nightclub. First he promised to dump his wife and their terraced Georgian home to "set her up in a condominium in New York. She actually believed that for a year." Then he said he would buy her a time-share in an apartment on the Costa Brava. "In two years they spent four days in London and a rugby weekend in Paris."

"Cathy attracts those kind of men," Emer said once. "It's some kind of masochism. I can't explain it."

Sometimes Emer says she believes Cathy just has a very strong gallivanting streak. Sometimes she calls her a mad bitch. And Cathy is pretty. Emer has to admit that. "I suppose that's part of her problem. But she's losing her looks. After thirty, things start to go wrong with your skin."

Now Cathy has moved to the country. She has taken a small house by a lake in the midlands. She lives there with Alan, whom she met when they were doing a ceramics course in Galway Regional Technical College some years ago. After graduating, they tried to get a business going in Galway city, but there was strong competition and they lost money. They wanted some place without many overheads or social distractions. Then Cathy remembered the lake houses. She had visited them as a child when they were 'white and gleaming by the waterside'. They had been built as potential holiday homes in the late sixties, but through one thing and another they never became viable. In recent years many of the houses had changed hands in quick succession. Nowadays, apart from a retired German doctor and his wife who live there all year round, nobody seems very sure who owns what.

Cathy and Alan are renting from a cousin of hers who spends most of the year in Dublin. They've fitted out an old boathouse as a workshop and Cathy has been working flat out, day and night, trying to finish a contract for the canteen of a local computer factory.

One day, out of the blue, Emer got a letter from Cathy to say that Alan would be spending most of August with his parents in England and wouldn't it be nice if both of us came down to stay. It was time we all got reacquainted, she said.

"Reacquainted is right," Emer said. "I mean, you know I haven't heard from her for almost a year."

"Let's go down," I said. We could bring the sailboards. We could swim and relax and do nothing for a few weeks. Besides, it would give Emer a chance to visit the places of her childhood.

"I want to see this country you're always talking about," I said.

"Oh, I'm sure it's not anything like the place I remember."

Sitting in the kitchen of Cathy's house late one evening, Emer talks about her father.

"The summer before Cathy was born Dad drove our Ford Prefect off the end of a pier out there on the far side of the lake. Mam used to say it was all the result of his drinking. But if you ask me it was other things as well. Anyway, he mustn't have been so serious about it. The water wasn't very deep and he managed to get out and up onto the shore. He sat there and waited for the sun to dry his clothes. He never got his shoes properly dried, though. He had to throw them out eventually. I think they must have taken the car out too but I don't ever remember seeing a Ford around the place. The first car I remember was a Volkswagen, a small black Beetle."

I wait for Emer to finish this story, but the conversation drifts on to other matters and I sit and look out at the lake water as it glows and then slowly darkens.

The weather is too calm for windsurfing. All day the lake glints and refuses to stir. In the morning, Emer and I go for long walks along the shore. One day I take a boat out and try some fishing, but it's too bright and the water is too clear to catch anything.

The next afternoon we row out to one of the islands and wander among the ruins of a seventh-century monastery. We have lunch, sitting on the grass by the water, and do our best to beat off the tiny flies that swarm in the heat. I try to get Emer talking about her parents. I want to know what happened back then.

"It's no secret. It's not something I'm trying to hide." She twists a blade of grass tightly around one of her fingers and stares out into the shimmering distance. "When I was ten and Cathy was seven, or maybe eight, my father just disappeared. Well, as far as we were concerned, he disappeared. Early one morning in the summer of 1965 he packed a suitcase and took off. Nobody had any idea where he'd gone to, although after a week or so people began to mention England or the States. For months, for the best part of a year, Mam contacted relatives on both sides of the family: in London and Liverpool and in Boston and New York and San Francisco. It was a terrible time. Every single day she cried quietly from morning to night. Eventually she stopped expecting news of any kind. Then she just gave up, in ways. As you can imagine, we had virtually no money. There wasn't much we could do about it, so after a year of this Mam sold the house and we rented a smaller place in town. But it wasn't just the money. It was people and the way they behaved and what they said. 'I don't understand these people,' she told me once. 'How can they be so cruel? It's not natural.' But it was natural. I've realised since that cruelty can come so naturally to people.

"Years later, after Mam had died, someone sent me a newspaper cutting from England. It was just this photograph taken at a union meeting of electrical engineers in Brighton. There was nothing else. And I knew, before I even examined that photograph, that my father was in it. He was right there in the back row, all dressed up and smiling, as if nothing had ever been wrong in the world."

Emer stops and looks at me. "I know you don't believe this."

"It's a weird story."

"It's a true story. It happened to us."

Every morning the first thing I do is check for a sign of wind, but by early afternoon the same dull heat smothers the lake and soon the flies have risen in a fine haze across the water. Cathy spends most of the day in the shed. Wearing a T-shirt and shorts, she emerges late in the afternoon. She sits in the shade, drinking chilled beer shandy, staring out at the stillness.

"Oh, the dog days of my childhood," she says, in her slow, languorous voice, "when the midlands smouldered and vanished."

Sometimes she lies on the back seat of the car, with all the doors thrown open, and plays tapes. She plays *Astral Weeks*, or early Bob Dylan, or, on particular evenings, any of those new batch of women country singers — Kathy Mattea, k d lang, Nanci Griffith. The sweet, whining sounds of these love-lorn country songs sends Emer into the kitchen, where she can be heard clattering about, pretending to be busy preparing dinner. Later in the evening we drink and talk and play cards — games where none of us can agree on the rules and which usually end without a winner.

"Alan would know the rules, I'm sure," Cathy says on one of these occasions. "Alan is invariably very good on the rules of things."

"You know, Dad was responsible for bringing electricity to this part of the country," says Emer. "He was one of the men the electricity board employed to visit the villages and townlands to convince people that they would have a better life if only they allowed this great power into their homes. He would call a meeting in the local hall wherever he was sent and try to impress them with the miracle that could be available at the flick of a switch. These country people, mostly small farmers, weren't easily convinced. If it meant change to them it meant money as well, and they didn't want to know about it. Some people were genuinely afraid. And some were just backward, I suppose. Of course the women were more prepared to listen. They saw how it could help bring an end to some of the eternal drudgery. Even Mam, even after he'd gone, whenever we had a power cut, would come out with 'May God bless your father. Without him places like this would still be in the dark ages.'"

"That was just something she said to keep up appearances," says Cathy. "Deep down she hated the bastard."

Cathy and Emer look at one another, neither of them prepared to go any further.

It's evening and Cathy and I are in the kitchen, drinking coffee. Emer has gone rambling— "It means to go and visit other people's houses," she explains, "people used to do it a lot in the days before television." She's gone to see a woman, an old primary-school teacher, whom she's not sure will recognise her after all these years.

"Come out with me," says Cathy. "I'll show you the shed. I'll potter in the pottery for you."

She pulls the bolt back and we step into the dimly lit workshop. The walls are lined on two sides by a double row of deep shelves on which are arranged various pieces of finished work—vases, jugs, pots, dishes. There's a table in the middle of the room covered in rows of unglazed cups. The kiln stands on a platform of bricks by the back wall. Cathy lights a cigarette and leans back against the table. Her red hair, pulled off her forehead, is tied up with a bright purple scarf. Her white T - shirt is covered with stains from the clay she's been working with all day. Her jeans are rolled up along her calves. Suddenly she goes over to the small back window and points out.

"Look across the lake. Somewhere over there you should be able to see the lights of Athlone shining on the water. On clear nights we could see them from our bedroom window. Mam would come in to tuck us into bed and she would often take us to the window first to look at those lights. I used to imagine there were millions of tiny boats with lanterns, anchored far out on the water. I can remember wondering why a grown-up could get so excited about the lights of a town in the distance."

Both of us stand there looking out, searching the darkening skyline for that twinkling from out of the past. It's almost quiet, but I think I can sense the movement of the water as it shifts about in the depths of the lake and we can hear the low waves slapping the shore. Then I realise I am listening to our breathing, close and rapid, and in no time I feel Cathy's body pressed against mine.

One night Cathy and Emer had a talk.

"We stayed up until God knows what hour and finished off the wine. We got a bit tipsy, I suppose. All the same, that Cathy gave me a fright."

Cathy told Emer that there might come a day when she would walk out into the lake.

"Just like that," she said. "'Walk out into the lake.' And she wasn't joking."

Cathy had said that as far as she was concerned, Emer and herself could never face things the way their mother had. Their mother had faith. She had a belief in a certain order of things, despite all that had happened. That was lost on them. They were shiftless, restless people. They had no centre.

"Cathy never had the full story about anything. Mam wasn't perfect. She had her day too.

"I found these letters—oh, years ago. After Mam died I had to sort through her things. Cathy wouldn't go near the place. Her clothes, her few bits of jewellery, her cookery books and all these novels and old magazines, all that sort of stuff. I found this bundle of typed letters, wrapped in old newspapers, in at the back of the wardrobe. They were all addressed to my mother and had been posted in Dublin back in the early sixties, in the days before Dad moved away. I didn't know what to do. I wanted to throw them out and I wanted to read them. So I glanced through one and thought that would be enough. I didn't even intend reading the whole thing. I checked for the sender's address but there wasn't any. There was something scribbled at the bottom of the page that I couldn't make out. So I read a few lines.

"I sat on the edge of the bed in my mother's old room in the middle of a September afternoon and read all twenty-three letters. They were love letters, of course, though not very much was said in any of them. But you could tell by the tone. You could tell from the way the writer talked about things in his everyday life. You could tell that very easily. He would say, I did this today, or tomorrow I'm going to visit such and such a person, and you could see why he was telling these things to my mother. He was sending the story of his life to her. And I suppose she did the same. They were two people in unhappy situations and they just kept the good things to tell to one another.

"A few times a year Mam would go up to Dublin. She'd be back in a day or two, laden down with bags from Arnotts and Switzers and summer or winter outfits for Cathy and myself. While she was away Dad would cope as best he could with feeding and entertaining us. He would tell us stories and make colcannon for dinner and jam sandwiches for tea. He'd take us with him on walks to neighbouring houses to collect milk or eggs.

"One night he brought me in to the station to meet Mam off the Dublin train. It was so cold. It must have been in January or February. I remember waiting and stamping up and down the platform, wearing my big furry mittens and my big woolly hat and Dad standing at the top of the platform. And every so often he would stamp his feet as well and say, 'It won't be long now.' Well, the train came in and we walked along, hand in hand, Dad looking into the brightly lit carriages, expecting to spot her. But she wasn't to be seen.

"After the train pulled out we walked around, searching. We looked in the waiting room and even asked a porter, but she wasn't anywhere in the station. So Dad said she must have missed the train or else she'd already gotten off and taken a hackney home. But when she wasn't at home he said she must have been carried on to the next station. This was the story they both stuck to when she reappeared the following afternoon. Mam said she'd fallen asleep and had been overcarried all the way to Sligo. You're really better off never finding out about people's secret lives. Especially your parents'."

Out the back Cathy is dowsing down the car. She moves to the shore and back, carrying a large yellow bucket. She's singing something, and every time she throws the water over the car she whoops.

Emer lights a cigarette and turns to watch her sister. "Cathy is like Mam. She has all this unhappiness hidden away."

A wind has been rising on the lake since morning and I reckon it should be good enough to keep us out for the afternoon. I shift the sailboards down from the roof of the car and take the rest of the gear from the boot.

The women are in the kitchen, talking. I go to the window and give a few raps on the glass. They both turn and look towards me.

"Come out," I shout. "Come out and try this for wind."

But I can see they don't want to have to hear me. They've been going back over old incidents and occasions, memories that would mean little or nothing to you or me. They sit there, caught between words, and I am an intruder, a boy at the window who hasn't realised that the game has now turned serious.

"Don't bother," I mouth, and shake my head. "It's all right."

As I turn and face out into the freshening wind I hear Cathy's laughter ringing out, carrying its joy across all these miles of land and water.

These Things Happen

Then she told him the story about the girl and the baby. There was this girl she knew who wanted to get rid of a baby. The girl was two months pregnant and she tried a few different ways, but none of them worked. She thought about having an abortion, and then she read somewhere about taking a hot bath and plenty of drink. So she tried it and she got very drunk and sick and that didn't work either. So then she forgot about the baby and didn't try to kill it anymore. And the girl had the baby, a boy. Now the baby is starting to walk and the girl is working and her boyfriend looks after him during the day. That was the story. It wasn't much of a story really, but he didn't say anything.

When she told him the story they were in the pub. It was a small pub. There was just one room with a long bar counter and there were a few tables and chairs at one end of the room. There was a wooden bench along the wall opposite the counter. They were sitting on the bench. It was early in the evening and there weren't many people around.

"Tell me the things you're afraid of," she said.

"What do you mean?" he said.

"You're afraid of dogs."

"What makes you say that?"

"I know," she said. "Even if a dog barks, if you're near, you jump."

"That's a bit of an exaggeration," he said, and he called the woman behind the bar and ordered two more drinks.

"I'd say you're afraid of other things too," the girl said.

"Everyone's afraid of something."

"Maybe," she said, though she didn't sound convinced.

They didn't speak for a while. A man at the counter said, "Oh, I'm the boy to please her" and another man laughed. And the woman behind the bar said something and both men laughed together.

Then the girl said, "Sometimes, I'm afraid."

"Why should you be afraid?" he said.

"I'm afraid of a lot of things," she said. "But sometimes I'm just afraid. Of nothing."

"But that's silly. It's silly to be afraid of nothing."

"It just happens."

"Are you afraid now?"

"No. Not now, but I could be anytime. I suppose it's anxiety."

"Anxiety?" he said. "What do you mean?"

"You know. Like time is passing me by and I've nothing to show. It can make you feel panicky."

"But Jesus," he said, "you're still young."

'The Last Rose of Summer' came on the radio which was playing on a shelf behind the bar. The woman turned up the volume; she closed her eyes and listened to the song.

"What do you want?" he said, after a few minutes.

The girl looked up at the rows of bottles behind the bar. "Well," she said, "I'd like a champagne cocktail to start with, and a glass of that green stuff, that crème de menthe, and some caviar on toast and a packet of peanuts, if you don't mind."

"You know what I mean."

She thought for a moment. "Well, first of all," she said, "I'd like to have lots of children."

"That's a bit old-fashioned, isn't it?" he said. "Nobody has a lot of brats nowadays."

"Why do you call them that?"

"What difference does it make what I call them?"

"It shows your attitude, that's all."

"What's wrong with my attitude?" he said.

"Work it out for yourself," she said.

He was up at the counter, ordering more drinks, when the man with the beard came in, pushing a go-car with a baby in it. The man left the go-car by a table near the door. He bought a bottle of beer and a Coke and took them back to the table. He poured some beer and drank it quickly. Then he gave the baby a glass with some Coke in it.

When the baby had finished, the man loosened the safety belt and lifted it out onto the floor. The baby stood by the go-car for a moment and then began to walk around.

The man sat at the table, drinking his beer and watching the baby. It was a fat baby with a red face and curly blonde hair.

"It's still very warm out," the man said, looking over at the couple. He rubbed his beard as he spoke.

"Yeah," said the girl. "It's hot, all right." She looked at the baby who stood blinking now in the sunshine of the open doorway. "You've a nice baby," she said.

"He's not bad when he's quiet," said the man, "but wait 'til he gets fed up."

"Oh," said the girl.

Three men and a woman came into the pub. Some were carrying musical instruments in cases. All four sat down around a table at the far end of the room. One of the musicians took a mandolin from a case and started to tune it.

Up at the bar, someone said, "I'm telling you, this is the best fucking country in the world."

When the baby started to cry, the man picked it up and held it in his arms. After a bit, the baby stopped crying and the man gave him another drink of Coke. He put the baby back down on the floor. The baby started to cry again.

"Oh, shut up," said the man, and he winked at the girl.

"I see what you mean," she said.

The woman behind the bar looked over at the man and at the baby standing bawling in the middle of the floor. "Whist, ya divil ya," she said, grinning at both of them.

The man finished his drink and stood up. He looked at the couple on the bench.

"I wouldn't mind," he said, "but we were just down on holiday for the week and my wife left me the other night and I haven't seen her since."

Then he picked up the crying baby and put it back in the go-car. He didn't say anything else. He just left, pushing the go-car ahead of him.

The girl watched him leaving; then she watched the empty doorway for a moment.

"That's terrible," she said. "Imagine, on holidays and with the baby and everything."

"Yeah, well," he said, "these things happen."

Details

My wife joined a writers' group. She wanted to write she said, but it was driving her out of her mind. She couldn't find the proper words to say what she had to say. She wasn't sure what good it would do, but she hoped that simply being in a room with a number of similarly intentioned people might at least help to clear her mind.

She was expecting too much, I thought. "What you've got to do," I said "is sit down somewhere on your own and write." She said, "Well, perhaps that's true." But she was going to give it a try, anyway.

The group met, once a week, in the back room of a pub in town. "A dark, dingy sort of place," she said and she didn't tell me anything else about it.

But there were indications that she was making some kind of break-through. And she was organised. She worked at a table by the window, in the living-room. Every morning she would place her typewriter carefully on the table and leave a small stack of paper beside it. She'd wait then until I'd left for work. I never caught her at it. She always kept the pages of whatever she was currently working on in a locked drawer of the bureau. Once, when I asked her how things were going, she said, "I'd prefer if you didn't question me about it."

Before all this my wife taught English and French for eight years in a girls' secondary school. She seemed quite happy for a long time and then, one year, she started to go quietly off the rails. It was the same year we tried to have a child.

She began by missing days. When I came home from work she would still be in bed, or else she would be sitting in the living-room in her bath robe, staring at the television. One evening I found her lying, half-dressed, in the bath, eating corn flakes from the box. There was an empty vodka bottle on the floor nearby. "Get me out of here. Please," she said in a sort of whisper.

That was the evening they brought her to the hospital. I can't even begin to understand what they do to you in there, but sometimes it seems to work. When she came out she was back to her old self, as far as I could tell. She wouldn't talk about it, though, and I was glad of that.

One evening she brought a friend home after a group meeting. I came in from the kitchen and saw a girl in blue jeans and black jumper standing by the bookshelves, examining the titles. "I bet you've never read even half this shit," she said in an American accent.

This was Claire. My wife introduced us, then went out to the kitchen to organise drinks.

"Well," Claire said, "I hear you're a writer too."

"No," I said. "I'm an accountant, I'm afraid."

"That's not telling me anything at all now, is it?" she said.

She sat down on the arm of the couch and idly turned the pages of a large paperback. She had straight blonde hair and it fell across part of her face so that she had to keep brushing it aside. She was young, about twenty-two or twenty-three. She looked like some kind of student to me.

My wife came in, carrying glasses, but nothing else. She'd heard us talking. "No, really," she said. "He used to write. In college." I wrote for the college magazine, but it was something I didn't want to remember.

"He's very good with my stuff, you know," my wife said.

"I bet," Claire said.

"I'm afraid we're fresh out of drinkables," my wife said and she looked at me.

I said I'd go down to the off-licence and get a bottle.

"Or two," she shouted after me as I pulled the hall door shut.

When I got back things weren't the same in the living-room. Someone had put on a Jimi Hendrix record and pushed the volume up. There was a particular smell in the air, the smell of cannabis.

My wife had a freshly lit cigarette in her hand. Claire was lying back on the couch, staring at something I couldn't see.

"Jesus," I said. "What's this?"

And my wife said, "This is let's get completely out of it at a quarter-to-eight in the evening time." And then, "Don't worry, darling. We're just trying to relax."

She held up the smouldering cigarette. "Try some," she said.

"Try it," Claire said. "It's really good. It will do you good. Really."

She said "really" in a slow voice, drawing the word out to three syllables. Re-al-ly.

I took the cigarette and had a drag, but illegal drugs never did anything for me.

I filled three glasses with wine and handed one each to Claire and my wife. I drank the first glass quickly. I stood at the window and looked up and down the road. Across the way a man was lying under a jacked-up bright red Toyota Corolla. I could see his legs sticking out. It was Mr Hayes, our neighbour, as far as I could tell. Farther up the road, some boys were playing a game of football. "Gift," one of them shouted, and another one waved his arms about wildly.

Claire and my wife were talking. About writing.

"After I've been working hard or something," Claire said, "I feel I want some violent sensation. I want to get drunk or really stoned. I want things to happen to me."

"I know exactly how you feel," my wife said. "I want something exciting."

"You know, you're sitting there for absolute hours trying to get the stuff onto the page and you're so worked up and so static at the same time."

"So what do you want?" my wife said.

And then they started this kind of talk I won't even bother repeating. They went on like that for a long time. It sounded clever, but I knew it was just dope talk. You can tell it a mile off. I stood by the window, hoping something would happen out there, and listening to my wife and that American girl. The strangers in my living-room. One of them kept playing Jimi Hendrix again and again. 'Purple Haze', 'Voodoo Chile', all that sixties' stuff.

Eventually, I went out to the kitchen for a whiskey. Then I went to bed. But I could hear them yapping down there until all hours.

Afterwards, the only thing my wife had to say about Claire was: "Claire is all right. She's quite a good writer. But I wouldn't call her the most stable person."

Around this time my wife's first published story appeared in a national newspaper. After I read it, I had to read it again. It was not the type of story I had imagined her writing. It didn't seem to be a woman's kind of story. She said, "You're out of touch with writing today. The last modern book you read was The New Testament."

She put the payment, which wasn't a lot, towards buying a Japanese wall-hanging for the kitchen. She wanted something to remember the occasion by. It's still there, above the dining counter, after everything.

About three months later she got another story into a literary magazine. I didn't read this one. I don't think we were even talking much by then. I didn't want to have to read a story to find out what was going on in our lives.

Late one Saturday evening the phone rang. It was the American girl, Claire, "Hi," she said. "Is anyone in?" I told her my wife was away for the weekend. She was attending a workshop at some literary festival down the country.

Claire said it was just that she had this manuscript and some books she wanted to return, and that she was flying out to Chicago in the morning to visit her dad for a month and would it be an awful bother if she dropped by, just for a split-second, with the stuff. "That's all right," I said. "Call around. I'm just sitting here waiting for something to do."

As a matter of fact I was hoping to clear a backlog of work over the weekend, but, so far, I hadn't made much progress with it.

I had a shave and changed my shirt. I poured some whiskey and left the bottle on the table. I turned on MTV and turned off the lights. After a while I switched to the late-night film.

I was beginning to doze off when the doorbell rang. She stood there in the light from the hall, with a package under her arm. You could see she'd been drinking.

"All right," she said, "tell me I'm late."

"That's OK," I said.

"Oh God," she said. "You wouldn't believe this, but I met these guys I hadn't seen in months and we got talking. And you know the way things get. So! Can I come in?"

She stepped by me into the hallway and I followed her into the living-room.

"Here's the books and stuff," she said. She put the package on the table.

She sat down on the couch and lit a cigarette. She was wearing a tight black woollen dress that rode a long way above her knee, black tights and black lace-up boots with short, pointed heels.

I poured her some whiskey and some for myself.

She took a sip. "So! How are you, Mr Accountant?" she said.

"I'm fine," I said.

I sat on the arm of the couch, then moved down onto the seat.

"That's right," she said, "make yourself at home."

"I'm trying," I said.

She looked around the room. On the television screen, dark-suited men in hats lurked in alleyways and chased one another across the roofs of skyscrapers.

"I love Edward G Robinson," she said. "He has such a calm, unperturbed face. I could watch him for hours."

I wasn't sure which of them was Edward G Robinson and I wondered how she, at her age, could know anything about these old films, but I said, "I can take him or leave him, I suppose."

"Really?" she said. "I'd say there are lots of things you could take or leave."

I pretended I hadn't heard that.

"Oh!" she said, as if she'd remembered something. "What about my face? Would you call that a calm, unperturbed face?"

She'd turned towards me. It was the first time I had seen her close up. She shook the hair back off her right cheek.

She said, "You can see America in my face. Do you believe that? That's what a boyfriend told me once. He was one real bullshitter." She smiled.

I could see her face in the flickering television light. She had blue or grey eyes, I couldn't be sure.

"What do you think?" she said.

I decided it was time for another drink.

She said, "I've maybe had too much to drink. But, like they say, maybe's not for sure."

She held out her empty glass and I poured the whiskey into it. As I was filling my own glass she slipped slowly from the couch, so she was sitting on the floor with her legs crossed beneath her. The upper part of her body then began to sway gently, to and fro, as if she were moving to music I could not hear. She had her eyes shut.

I was standing by the table, watching this, when she said, "I see that look you're giving me."

"What look is that?" I said.

I moved back over and sat on the arm of the couch, near her.

"The look you've been giving me all along," she said.

"It's no look in particular," I said.

"Oh, yes it is. I know that look."

"What kind of look is it?"

"It's the look that says 'I want to see you with your clothes off, Claire.'"

"Is it?" I said.

"Yes, it is. You've got that exact look."

She stood up. She stood in front of me, blocking the television screen.

"I am going to take my clothes off now. That is, if you don't mind."

I shook my head.

"I will start down here."

She bent down and undid the laces of each boot. She raised her left foot and I realised she was looking for my help. Then, in her stocking feet, she moved nearer to me, near enough so I could touch.

"You are learning things tonight," she said. "Isn't that right? I can see you are."

I was running my fingers slowly along the back of her calf, over the ever so slightly rough material of her tights.

"We should learn something new every day, I suppose," I said.

"Oh, yes, we should," she said. "I think we are all learning something here tonight. What is it exactly I am learning, would you say?"

She smiled. Another look had come into her eyes. I didn't pay any attention to it. I moved my hand across her knee and up along the inside of her thigh.

"I don't know. What are you learning?" I said.

"Well," she said. "First off, I am learning how a man can be unfaithful to his wife. That is most definitely something every woman needs to learn, don't you think?"

She'd closed her legs on my hand. It was warm there.

"You wouldn't want to do that now," she said. "Would you? Think about it."

She opened her legs the smallest bit. I pulled my hand away.

She reached over, picked the packet of cigarettes up off the floor, shook one out, lit it and sat on a chair by the table. I heard her say— "This is what I call an interesting situation. Wouldn't you call this a really interesting situation?" She crossed her legs and waited.

Across the room, strange things were happening on the television screen. It wasn't difficult for me to believe that such strange things were happening.

One day my wife said to me: "You know, there are many things in this world which neither of us have ever experienced." She could come out with statements like this on occasion. Somehow, her statements always made me feel uneasy.

It was the beginning of the time before my wife moved away. During that time she no longer did very much writing. She would leave the house early in the morning and not return until late in the evening. She must have spent a lot of her day in town. She bought a lot of clothes and accessories. There would be large paper bags with exotic names on them scattered around the bedroom. "What does this mean?" I wondered.

When she said, "We really have to talk," I knew what she meant. The circumstances could not be ignored any longer.

My wife went to live on an island off the west coast. There were other writers living there, and artists and people who did pottery and that kind of thing. How do I know where she was? She sent me a postcard. On the front was a picture of a boat with dark sails moving through a mist. On the back was written: "Here I am, Anne (your wife)." The writing was not distinct and "your wife" had been penned in blue by somebody else. I imagine she wrote and posted it one night when she'd been drinking.

After that she seemed to disappear. Maybe she went to the States—to New York or California—places she often talked about. Perhaps she stayed in the West and set up a colony or one of those artists' communes, but I doubt it. There are people like that, but my wife isn't one of them.

Next thing I heard she had a job in television, producing children's programmes. That could be like her, all right, I thought and I wondered what had happened to the writing. Had the writing gone out the window?

Recently I came across this story quite by accident. It was in an upmarket women's magazine I was leafing through in the doctor's waiting-room. The magazine was more than a year out of date.

The story was called 'Details' and, in it, a man and the man's wife's friend have a brief, unsatisfactory affair. There's a scene towards the end where the wife's friend (who's really a girl, it must be said) leads the man on in a very strong way. The man is frustrated and when, finally, the girl refuses to have anything to do with him he beats her badly about the face and body. It's not very clear, in the end, whether he goes any further, but it's hinted at.

Of course, the reason I read this story in the first place was because my wife had written it. I read it again. I read through parts of it a third time. It was full of details, just like the title said. It was quite a plausible story. I recognised that man; I recognised that girl.

I tore the pages from the magazine, folded them up and stuck them in my pocket. As I sat there, I realised revenge can take a long time. Sometimes, when you think you've escaped, it's been there all along, just waiting to ambush you.

Ciao, Bella

What he said, she didn't understand. But she knew what was coming next. She saw the brown feet and legs, the towel being spread on the sand beside her. She didn't turn to face him until he tapped the back of her left knee. He wanted a cigarette, it seemed. She shook her head and turned a page of the magazine. He was sitting on the towel, stretching his legs. This time he touched her shoulder, quickly.

"*Mi chiamo Carlo*," he said.

She turned another page.

"My name is Carlo," he said.

She said nothing.

"*Francese?*" he said. "*Inglese?* You are English?"

She shook her head.

"*Inglese*. Yes, English." He motioned towards the magazine.

"No," she said. "No *Inglese*."

She gathered up a handful of gravelly sand. She let the stones and the smooth fragments of glass slip through her fingers. She turned over onto her back and looked out towards the sea.

He took a cigarette from a packet and lit it. He leaned over on his left elbow, looking at her.

"What are you called? Your name?" he said, pointing at her with the cigarette.

She said, "My name is none of your business."

He pulled on the cigarette and said, "Where is your *amica?*"

"My friend is at the hotel," she said.

"Which is the hotel?"

She pointed vaguely in the direction of the prom. "My boyfriend is at the hotel. He is minding the baby. He is coming down soon, very soon."

He smiled. He said, "What is the name of this baby? This baby, what do you call it?"

"Carmen," she said. "Her name is Carmen."

"*Ah, bella,*" he said.

She thought perhaps the name was a mistake. It didn't sound convincing. She was sure he realised there was no baby. But he asked no more questions.

When he'd gone she went for a swim. She came back and sat on the edge of the towel. She watched the sea and the boats and, over beyond, the green and grey mountains.

When she woke she heard the sounds of the sea and the people, and the clock chiming in the distance. She counted the number of chimes. It was a quarter-to-twelve. She sat up. Her stomach was turning red. She spread factor four on the sore skin. She was hot and she was thirsty.

On her way back from the drinking tap, she saw them walking along the prom—her husband and the English girl—carrying a bag of shopping each. They crossed the railing and came down the steps. The English girl spotted her first, and shouted "Hi" and waved. The English girl said, "I picked him up in the supermarket, trying to find the cheese counter."

And he grinned and showed her the bag with the food in it. "You're getting burnt," he said.

They ate the bread with cheese and tomatoes, while the English girl had some yogurt. Then they had a nectarine each. Afterwards, they all lay in the sun. The English girl lay somewhat apart, but within talking distance. She turned over at regular intervals and spent a lot of time in swimming. They watched the English girl from the beach as she waded through the water.

"Tell me," she said. "Do you think she's pretty?"

"No. Not really pretty," he said. "But she's not bad."

And later on he said, "She has a big arse."

On the first day, the very first thing the English girl had said to her was, "I see you forget your bikini top, then." Well, she never had one actually, but she said yes, she had, and the English girl said, "What a pity. I'm afraid I've nothing I could lend you."

They were in the water, the English girl in her black one-piece and sunglasses and she wearing a bikini bottom and bra. She wore the bra because, as far as she could see, no one went topless here. It was a place for families.

The English girl's name was Alex. She lived in London and worked for the BBC. She'd been to Germany and Switzerland and was spending the last week of her holiday in Italy.

Alex said, "See that man over there, the sleazy one over by the boat?"

A middle-aged man was sitting on the side of one of the boats which had been pulled up onto the beach. He was staring in their direction.

"That creep has been eyeing me all morning. He just persists in staring. The old pervert just stands about and stares."

Now the man was smiling to himself. He didn't look quite right.

"I'm staying at this really grotty ponseeown," said Alex. That's how she said it: pon-see-own. She described how the brother of the man who ran the *pensione* hung around the hallway. And each evening he would accost her on her way in from the beach and ask her to go for a drive in his Fiesta.

"You know what that means," she said. "The men down here are so sleazy, it's unbelievable."

Alex's mouth made a funny shape when she said the words "sleazy" and "unbelievable." But when Alex took off her sunglasses as they were leaving the water, you could see that she had very nice eyes.

Alex said, "You're not newly-weds, are you? Are you really? Oh gosh, I'd never have thought."

They were in the water again. Up on the beach a man, her husband, lay asleep in the shade of a boat.

Alex said, "Didn't you miss all the excitement you'd have had at home, then? I mean Rome is nice, but I think I'd rather like all that stuff with pissed uncles and boring aunts and all those embarrassing speeches and things."

At first her mother had said, "Well, it's none of our business now, is it?" And another time, "If you want to deprive your father and myself of the big day, well, go ahead."

Her mother had said other things too. The last time they met it was: "You're not still going ahead with this farce, are you?"

A long time ago now, it seemed, she had told him she was pregnant.

"You can't be serious," he said.

But she was.

"What are you going to do about it?" he said.

"To do?" she said.

"We can't spoil things now," he said. He spoke calmly, but she could see that he was frightened.

"There's only the one thing you can do," he said.

She did it. The only thing.

He was tired again that night. She listened to him snoring and then she listened to the noises of the traffic echoing in the courtyard down below. Later, when she woke, it was raining heavily. She went to the window and leaned out. She rubbed her wet hand across her forehead. She stood there, watching the rain, waiting for it to stop. Eventually she went back to bed.

In the morning the courtyard and streets were dry again. She didn't mention the rain. She thought maybe she'd dreamt it.

His toothache started on the Saturday morning of the holiday weekend. It was the *caffè latte* they'd had for breakfast he said. They searched for a chemist but, because of the holiday, all the shops in the town were shut. The woman in the *pensione* gave him some Anadin. They went to the beach, but, in the afternoon, the pain got worse and he returned to the *pensione* to try to sleep it off.

She spent the evening on the beach with Alex. They swam and talked and lay in the sun.

Later, when she told him Alex was going to Capri the next morning and that she'd asked them to come along, he said, "You go. Go on. It's all right."

'Who's That Girl?' was the song Alex selected on the jukebox. The waiter brought them ice-cream and, afterwards, coffee and more wine.

They had had a good day on the island. They had seen everything there was to see. "Isn't it fabulous?" Alex had kept saying.

The air out in the bay had been cooler, less deadening than at the beach. Coming back into the harbour, the town lay stretched, silent along the water, the mountains behind turning a faint shade of ochre. Back at the *pensione*, her husband was probably still sleeping it off. "You must try this restaurant," Alex had said, "I simply insist."

Anyway, here she was. She put on Alex's straw hat and Alex took her photo. Then she took Alex's photo. Alex wearing sunglasses, Alex without sunglasses.

The waiter came over and said, "Ladies, what would you like now?" so they ordered more wine.

Alex tried to play the same song on the jukebox again, but she pressed a wrong number and got an Italian ballad instead. It was getting dark. There seemed to be a lot of empty bottles on the table.

Then Alex was asking her questions—questions she didn't want to answer. She noticed the clock on the railway station tower across the square. "Oh, it's late," she said. "I have to go back."

But Alex was saying, "You know, you have lovely eyes. You really have the loveliest eyes."

It was evening. She lay on the beach, her eyes shut, listening to the men singing. Songs from operas she thought. Songs from old Italian operas with strange names. Beyond the voices she heard the sea, shifting slowly across the gravel.

"One day soon," she thought, "I will be back walking in a city in the rain."

The men were talking now. She heard the rising voices, the quickening rhythm of their speech. They were talking about mysterious and wonderful things. She was sure they were.

Here she is, some months later. It's almost Christmas and she's with a friend at a party. She's remembering how it happened. She says, "You don't think I'm exaggerating all this, do you?"

"No," says the friend, "I don't think you are. I wouldn't say you're exaggerating at all."

A Change in the Weather

It was my mother speaking. She was telling my father he should change his suit. They were in the kitchen. "It looks a bit shabby," she said. "Put on your really good suit, why don't you? But hurry up."

I was sitting on the back door step, trying to unravel a fishing line. The line lay in a pile on the ground and I was winding it around a wooden slat. Beside it, on the ground, was a small tin box with hooks and a penknife in it. I'd found the knife in the shed. It was rusty and blunt. My mother didn't know about it. The tin box was an old Oatfield sweet box that I used to keep stamps in before.

When my father had gone upstairs to change, my mother called me in. She was taking a tray of scones from the oven. She cut a scone in half, buttered both halves, put them on a saucer and handed it to me. I held the saucer, waiting for all the butter to melt.

"We'll be going soon," she said. "You're a big boy now and I want you to look after things. Remember everything I told you?"

I remembered what she'd told me earlier that morning. To be sure I was here when Aunt Julia called. To always call Aunt Julia by her proper name. Not to complain at meal-times. Not on any account to use bad language. If anyone called looking for my father, to say he'd be back in a few days.

"And don't be fighting with your brother," she said. "Remember you're older."

She sat on the couch in the living-room and began to brush her hair. She sorted through things in her handbag. My brother came and stood by the doorway watching. When she was ready she called him over and gave him a kiss.

Then she went out to the car where my father stood waiting with all the doors open because of the heat. They waved and shouted goodbye and we stood at the gate and watched the car until it turned the corner at the end of our road.

My brother stepped onto the first bar of the gate and started to hum to himself. I caught him around the waist and tickled him. He laughed and struggled to get free. I kept on tickling him and he slipped down onto the cement path. He was still laughing. When he stopped laughing he lay there and said, "I've a pain in my tummy."

"Softy," I said.

Later on Aunt Julia came. She wanted to know at what time my parents had gone. She asked if my mother had left any message. Then she went looking for my brother and found him playing with stones, in amongst the trees behind the shed.

When we were all in the kitchen, she said, "Now, I'm sure you're going to be good boys." And I said yes and went into the living-room to find a book to read. My brother stayed in the kitchen and Aunt Julia got him to help her wash the potatoes.

While she was getting ready the dinner my Aunt sang 'Que Sera Sera'. Then she tried to teach it to my brother. But my brother wasn't interested. He had his own songs. He sang

'Whiskey on a Sunday'. And then 'Cool Clear Water', which he'd learnt from one of my father's 78s.

"Oh, you only know drinking songs, you scallywag," my Aunt said.

"They're just songs," he said.

For dinner we had chops and potatoes and cabbage. It was the same as we usually had except Aunt Julia made a kind of gravy for the meat. The gravy was too salty and I scraped it off the chop, but my brother said, "I don't like this stuff," and he wouldn't eat any more. Aunt Julia told him to stay at the table until everyone was finished.

My brother said, "When is Mammy coming back?"

"When she gets the baby," Aunt Julia said.

After a bit my brother said, "Where do they get the babies from?"

"Babies are given by God," Aunt Julia said.

"Why don't you get God to give you a baby?" my brother said.

I looked at my Aunt. All she said was, "Look how your brother ate up all his dinner."

All that evening I sat in the shade and waited for the man called Kicker Kennedy to call to take me fishing. I unwound the rest of the line. Then I dug for worms. After I had twenty I gave up.

When nobody came I went looking for birds' nests in the hedges around the garden. There were hardly ever any and I didn't find one this time.

The next day we were playing football. Aunt Julia came out to the garden.

She said, "Well boys, you have a new baby sister."

"What's her name?" said my brother.

"You'll have to wait and see," she said.

"What's her name? Butter and grain," my brother shouted, kicking the ball into the hedge.

That night Aunt Julia said, "Say a special prayer for your Mammy. And one for your new sister too." I wondered what kind of prayer you should say for a baby, but eventually I thought of something.

I had forgotten about fishing when Kicker Kennedy called to the house. I was planning on building a tree-house before my parents came home, and I was looking through a hobby book for instructions, when he knocked on the back door and came in. He didn't see me at first. He spoke to Aunt Julia who was sitting by the range.

"Any news?" he said, and Aunt Julia shook her head. When he saw me he said, "How's the soldier?" He always called me that.

"What about the fishing?" he said.

When we were leaving Aunt Julia didn't say "Mind your sandals" or "Don't get wet." She sat in the living-room, waiting for something.

Kicker Kennedy lived by the lake. He lived there with his sister, and a boy my father said was his nephew, but the boys in school called him other things.

The first day we went on the lake my father came with us. While we sat with the lines in the water, the Kicker sang songs.

Songs I'd heard on the radio, like 'The Black Velvet Band' and 'The Streets of Baltimore' and other songs, like 'A White Sport's Coat and a Pink Carnation' and 'The Yellow Rose of Texas'. When he didn't know all the words he'd make something up. He'd put on an American accent. "This is a real hurtin' song," he'd say and start 'He'll Have to Go'. My father would listen, but he wouldn't sing. He'd look at me and smile.

On this day the Kicker didn't sing. He asked me riddles instead. "What's the biggest and most obvious thing in the world and yet nobody can see it?" What was it? I can't remember.

He told me a story. It was a long story about something that happened in America and I soon lost interest. I watched the water and hoped a fish would bite. The lake was flat and empty. Through the haze in the distance I could see small islands with stone walls and bushes. At the end of the story Kicker Kennedy said, "Just goes to show you. There are some people who have all the luck and some who can never get any."

We fished all that evening. We caught twenty-five perch and we almost caught a pike. "The next time," the Kicker said, "we'll get one."

My brother was up at the back of the garden, gathering armfuls of grass and piling it in a heap. He didn't see me. In the coal shed I spread the fish on a newspaper and arranged them according to size. I looked at their damp bodies, their blueness in the dim light.

I went into the house. Aunt Julia was standing by the living-room window, looking out. She knew I was there, but she didn't turn around.

"What's wrong?" I said.

"Sit down on the couch," she said.

"It's to do with your Mammy," she said.

What I remember most about the hospital is the whiteness; all the walls glaring in the room where they kept my mother. But she wasn't my mother anymore.

"Your Mammy's gone," Aunt Julia had said. Why was she saying these things to me? I looked at my father. I wanted him to say something. Aunt Julia took me outside. She said, "Be a good boy. Your Daddy needs your help now."

My sister wasn't brought home until after the funeral. The cot was put in the living-room during the day. She cried a lot. My brother stood at the end of the cot and watched her.

"What's her name?" he said.

But she didn't have a name yet.

Aunt Julia came most days. I'd hear her talking as she worked about the house. She said she couldn't let things go to rack and ruin. She said there was no point in just moping.

I kept out of the house. Mostly I sat on the ground in a cool place amongst the cypress trees and tried to think of things to do. I would hear all the sounds of traffic and of people coming and going on the road outside. Sometimes I fell asleep.

It was evening. We were in the living-room; the three of us sitting at the table. The cot was in the corner. The baby was crying. I wanted to tell my father to pick up the baby and stop her crying. But he was in a bad mood. He was always in a bad mood now. And Aunt Julia was busy in the kitchen. She brought in a dish of potatoes and served dinner. She didn't go near the cot. Maybe she was pretending she couldn't hear the crying. Everybody started to eat.

After a while, Aunt Julia said, "Isn't it time she was baptised? What are you going to call her?"

My father didn't answer.

"Didn't Helen have a name in mind?" she said.

My father put down his knife and fork. He hit his fist hard against the table. "Get out," he shouted. "Stop fussing around here and go home to your own bloody husband."

Afterwards, my father sat at the table, the knife and fork and the plate before him. My brother sat on the edge of the couch. For a long time the baby wouldn't stop crying. But it was as if she wasn't there anymore. She was like some found thing, without a name, that everyone had forgotten.

It got darker. Nobody turned on the light. My brother fell asleep. My father stared at the window as if expecting some sign of a change in the weather. But nothing stirred outside.

Then he started to speak in a low voice.

"Damn you," he said. "Damn you to hell."

He said it, over and over, to himself, quietly, in that house, with the night coming in and all of us gathered around in the darkness.

Start Of A Great Adventure

The first time Frank saw the new tenants they were kissing on the stairs in the dark. He was on his way in from work, and as he shut the hall door, he heard a low moaning sound coming from the landing. He turned and saw two bodies outlined against the glass panels of the door to Miss Fanning's office. They hadn't noticed him and he slipped down to the basement without putting on the light. Frank never mentioned this incident to Brenda, but despite all that happened later it was the most persistent memory he had of Peter and Nadine.

When he did bring up the new tenants in conversation the next morning, Brenda said, "They're nice, I suppose. They're only kids, though, and I'll tell you one thing, there isn't any way they're married."

"Not that it matters," Frank said.

"Oh Frank, it doesn't matter in that sense," Brenda said. "It just means they're not telling the truth, that's all."

Since Brenda became caretaker many years earlier, the tenants in the top-floor flat had changed almost yearly. They were usually students or student-types with jobs in advertising or journalism and Frank never cared much for any of them. His job as projectionist in a small downtown cinema meant he worked irregular hours, sometimes leaving home at eleven in the morning and returning after midnight. He hardly ever met any of the tenants and he kept what Brenda called "a safe distance" from the goings-on in the house.

Brenda's work was basic maintenance. She hoovered the stairs, washed the hallway, sorted the post, left out the rubbish for collection. She had keys to the offices and cleaned them during the slack midweek evenings. Generally, she kept an eye on things and Frank soon began to hear details on the new tenants.

Peter worked for a video production company and Nadine did something in computers. Nadine was cheerful. She would always stop for a chat. But Peter was moody and would hardly ever say a word. They came and went at all hours. They had the life of Reilly and probably didn't know it.

All this was of little interest to Frank, but occasionally he would remember the two people on the darkened landing and wonder about their secret life together.

After some weeks, Brenda began to complain. One morning she found three overflowing refuse sacks stinking out the top landing. Someone kept leaving the hall door open at lunchtime and the people in the offices were worried about bag-snatchers and thieves. And what's more: Peter's bike was an almost permanent eyesore in the hallway.

At work Frank spent most of the day in the projection room, running films, loading and reloading reels, servicing out-of-date equipment. In between shows he would run across the street and buy coffee and sandwiches to take away.

Sometimes he would meet his employer Trench on the stairs, and Trench would ask him into the office. "Have a barney," Trench would say. "Get it all off your chest." And Frank would talk about the weather for a few minutes and leave.

Trench's office was an old storeroom built into a corner of the stairwell so it had only three walls and no window. There was a broken-down projector and a pile of empty reels and then a desk and two straight-backed chairs. Trench never seemed to stop smoking and the smoke seeped out and gathered in the stairway. Every time Frank went by the office, he would cough loudly and hope Trench might get the message.

One afternoon Frank was passing through the foyer on his way in for the first show of the day. Carol, the girl who worked the ticket desk midweek, called him over and asked him to stand in for a second. She came back ten minutes after the programme was due to have started and said, "Don't worry, it's all right. Honest." She smiled, and as she brushed past him Frank caught the fuggy smell of Trench's office mixed in with Carol's skin smell. Trench was about Frank's age, maybe a bit younger. He was married and had a few children. Frank wanted to let him know he had him sussed, but he doubted if something like that would bother Trench.

Peter and Nadine had been in the flat about a month when, late one Friday night, Frank heard a loud sound from upstairs. At first he thought it was thunder.

"My God," Brenda said. "A herd of elephants, if you don't mind."

But things got worse. All that night doors slammed and people came and went, shouting and laughing. A dull beat pulsed through the house until the early hours. Sometime after six Brenda got dressed and said she was going to take a look. She found half-empty bottles and cans scattered along the stairs. Someone had vomited just inside the hall door and somebody had managed to scrape pizza topping along the entire length of the banister. A used condom hung on the rim of the bowl in the second floor toilet. Brenda said this was the straw that broke the camel's back.

The following afternoon, Brenda took Frank up through the house. Nothing had been touched. "You see," she said. "This is the kind of people we're dealing with."

Then she called up to the flat. Peter stuck his head around the door. He was really sorry, he said. Things had just gotten a bit wild. They would make sure everything was spick and span by the morning.

"He looks like he's on drugs or something," Brenda told Frank. "He looks weird."

"There's no law against that," Frank said.

The next day Nadine presented Brenda with a big bunch of flowers and a box of chocolates, but months later Brenda was still finding fragments of dried-in pizza on the carpet on the stairs.

Sometimes, as he watched people wandering in for the afternoon shows, Frank would spot a boy sauntering down the aisle or sitting with both legs thrown across the seat in front and be reminded of his son. Once he had followed someone out of the cinema and across the street to the coffee shop. But the boy changed his mind and left while Frank was ordering.

One day, when his son was fourteen years old, Brenda said, "I have to tell you that boy is a thief and a liar. I'm telling you because more than likely you'll never find out for yourself."

Frank was shocked that his wife should think of himself in this way. But she was right. He had as much idea about the boy as about the motion of the planets. His son was a well-kept secret to him.

For months he watched in silence as the boy's room filled up with stolen items—pieces of stereo equipment, books on chartered accounting and chemical engineering, pairs of outsize jeans and expensive runners—and he felt he had been hard done by. He said to Brenda, "What do you expect a person to do?"

Eventually Frank tried to talk to his son about it, but he couldn't finish a sentence without flying into a rage. When, unknown to Brenda, he went to the Gardaí he believed he had done something positive at last. The Garda sergeant didn't seem to take the matter very seriously. "He'll grow out of it" was what he said.

Then the boy started missing days at school, hanging out in amusement arcades in town, coming home smelling of cider and cigarette smoke. The school principal called Frank and Brenda in.

"It seems your son is angry at the world," the principal said.

At night Frank would listen to his son moving about his bedroom or hear him crying out in his sleep and he would sense his own strength and hope draining out of him.

When he was sixteen the boy left home and went to live in a squat in London. A year later a friend of his wrote to say that he had joined a religious sect and was living in the south of Spain. Every Easter since an unsigned card would arrive, asking if they would like to make a contribution to the upkeep of the community. They never discussed these requests but Frank was sure Brenda posted money out a few times a year.

Whenever Frank heard the word Spain he would think of a flat landscape with a shaven-headed boy in a long bright robe hurrying through a distant haze of heat.

The problem with the water started in October. Brenda told Frank that someone had been messing with the pump which had been installed four years earlier to get water to the top of the house whenever the mains pressure ran low. But the pump made an annoying high-pitched sound and Brenda had always arranged with tenants to have it on for a few hours every morning and evening when water was most needed. Now, she said, it was being put on at all hours—at lunchtime, in the middle of the afternoon, at ridiculous times. The people in the offices complained about the noise. All Brenda could do was turn it off. But then Peter or Nadine would come back down and turn it on again. "What are they doing up there at three o'clock in the day?" Brenda asked.

She began to find notes on the hall table in the morning or pushed under the door late in the afternoon asking her to please leave on the pump.

She showed the notes to Frank. He thought they were reasonable. "After all," he said, "it is very high up."

"That isn't the point," Brenda said. "It isn't only about water."

Late one night, Frank heard the basement door creak open and then the pump came on. He checked the time; it was half-past two.

"See what I mean?" Brenda said. "They're trying to provoke me. They want to force me out of the job."

"Not at all," Frank said.

"Oh, yes," she said. "Of course, you never see anything. Even what's right under your nose."

Frank lay in bed, trying to sleep, but the whine of the water pump seemed like a warning of trouble in his life.

At Christmas the cinema shut for a few days and the offices took a week's break. On Christmas Eve morning Frank saw Nadine hauling a large suitcase along the street. He waved to her but she was searching the traffic for a taxi and didn't see him.

Frank went to the pub at four o'clock. He wanted to get drunk, but he wound up talking to a fat man in a suit at the bar who insisted on buying him a gin and tonic.

"You know, every Christmas I start drinking at precisely five o'clock on the twenty-third and I never stop until it's all over. I never stop," the fat man said. "And I'll tell you something. It works. It bloody well works."

On St Stephen's day, Brenda went to visit an aunt and Frank stayed in and watched 'Casablanca' on the video. Late in the afternoon, he thought he heard a noise from the top of the house. He took Brenda's bunch of keys and climbed the stairs, stopping on every landing to listen and to check under the doors for light. When he reached the top landing he sat down on the steps and lit a cigarette. The house was empty. He could hear the attic door rattling in the wind and the sound of an alarm from somewhere on the street. He sat there for a while and finished another cigarette. Then he went through the keys in the bunch and found the two for Peter and Nadine's flat.

When he opened the door he got the stench of rotting rubbish. He pulled up the window in the lounge and turned on the light. The place was in a mess. In the bedroom two single beds had been pushed together to make one. There were clothes everywhere. The bedroom walls were covered in some kind of painting that looked faintly unpleasant to Frank though he wasn't sure why.

He went into the bathroom and had a piss. He flushed the toilet. He ran both taps in the bath and rinsed it out. In the hallway he found the immersion switch and flicked it on. Then he went downstairs to get a bathtowel and soap. Back in the lounge he examined the things that were scattered about on the table. He found an unopened Christmas card from Australia and read it. He took a glass from the draining board and poured some brandy from a bottle on the sideboard. Then he sat in an armchair by the fireplace and waited.

As he was leaning down to pour another drink he noticed something white and crumpled on the floor near one of the dining chairs. He reached over and picked it up. It was a roll-your-own cigarette. He broke open the paper and smelt the contents. He spread some on the palm of his hand and examined the thin dark fibres scattered through the lighter-coloured tobacco. Frank had seen the college boys who checked the tickets on the late shows smoking joints. He had watched them grin at the customers as they came in and he had heard them giggling in the foyer after the film had started. He shoved the mixture back into the paper and stuck it in his box of Rothmans.

He sat in the bath for half-an-hour, topping up with hot water every so often. Afterwards he checked the taps in the kitchen. He rinsed the bath and flushed the toilet again. There didn't seem to be any problem with water.

When he had all but finished the brandy Frank took another quick look around the flat. He washed the glass and put the bottle back on the sideboard. When he was satisfied that everything was more or less as he'd found it, he shut the window, switched off the lights and left.

Frank was in the projection room one night when he remembered the roll-your-own cigarette. He had hidden it behind a stack of spare reels, just in case Trench was snooping around. The film had started and there was time to kill. He twisted the torn end and lit up. He watched the smouldering paper and waited for the sweet smell to reach him. When he took his first drag he inhaled deeply. He watched the smoke curl and diffuse in the white beam that shot out into the auditorium. He felt something rise in his chest and then stop. As the foreign voices on the soundtrack grew clearer, he tried to piece an image to each sound. But soon he lost interest in the film and stared up at the smoke particles shifting in and out of light. He waited for something to happen.

Suddenly the room seemed warm and clammy. He opened the door and brought his stool to the doorway. Trench and Carol were down in the foyer, talking. He felt no sensation now except tiredness as he listened to the voices falling and rising.

When Frank woke, the reel was spinning wildly and the house lights were still down, though the auditorium was empty. The smell of cannabis lingered in the air and he emptied the ashtray on his way to the foyer. There was no sign of anyone out front and the main door was locked. Frank knocked at the office. Carol answered. She was smiling and when he told her he was locked in, she said, "Well now, that's terrible" and smiled again. Then Trench appeared and went down to let him out. "Get a good night's rest," Trench said, but Frank pretended he hadn't heard.

The next afternoon, as he was passing through the foyer, Carol winked and said, "Woo Frank, you're a dark horse." Frank tried to work out why he was the one who could be made to feel guilty over the whole business. He wondered if perhaps things were getting to him. He was nearly fifty years of age and most of the people he knew seemed to be dope smokers and liars.

For months there had been no trouble with the water. Brenda hardly ever mentioned Peter or Nadine. She complained about the weather instead. She ate a lot and began to put on weight. Occasionally, Frank would see Peter at the supermarket check-out or get the scent of Nadine's perfume in the hallway in the morning.

One night after work he met Peter at the hall door. Frank said good night and Peter mumbled something and started to climb the stairs. Suddenly he stopped and turned. "How about coming up for a drink, Frank?" he said.

Frank could see Nadine further up, leaning over the banister. "No, I don't think so," he said. "Not tonight."

"No, seriously. Come on. You mightn't get the chance again."

Nadine waved. "Hi," she shouted. "Hi, Frank."

"Come on," Peter said.

"All right," Frank said. "Just for a minute. I'm bunched."

"Great," Peter said. "Nadine, make waves. We have a guest."

In the flat Nadine told Frank to sit down and Peter began to fix the fire.

"What's your poison?" Nadine asked him. "Let's see, we have beer, gin, whiskey."

"Promise us one thing though," Peter said. He turned and looked at Frank for a second. "Don't ask for water."

Peter laughed and Nadine made a strange giggling sound.

"No," Frank said. "I get the joke. Beer will do grand."

Nadine handed him a can of Heineken.

Frank noticed some black-and-white photographs scattered about on the coffee-table. They were pictures of Nadine, close-ups of her face, and they had the grainy quality of old magazine prints.

"What do you think?" Peter asked. "In your line of work and all."

Frank picked up a photograph. "They're good," he said.

"They're chronic," Nadine said.

"No they're not," Peter said.

"They are bloody awful," Nadine said. "Tell him what you really think of them."

Frank picked up another print.

"Don't mind her," Peter said. "It's PMT."

Nadine lay back in the chair and stretched out her legs, trying to aim a kick at Peter's knees. "You bastard," she said.

Peter grabbed both her feet and twisted them slowly.

"Peter, stop," she screamed. "Peter."

"Tell him the truth," Peter said.

"OK. He's really a genius," Nadine said. "Now, please let me go."

"That's it," Peter said and he let go of her legs.

Nadine sat up straight. "And he loves me. Isn't that right?"

"No," Peter said, "I don't."

"Oh yes, you do. You liar."

Peter looked at Frank. He was grinning. "Nadine, where's the stuff?"

"What stuff?"

Peter had moved behind Nadine's chair and was running his fingers through her long dark hair. "You know, the stuff Shane brought us."

"Oh shit," Nadine said. "Not now, Peter. We have company."

"Frank will join us. Won't you Frank?"

Frank shrugged his shoulders. "Maybe I'd better be going."

"Oh, no," Nadine said. "Stay. Do. Really. Don't mind us."

"Of course Frank'll stay," Peter said. "Now, get the stuff."

"All right," she said, "but only if Frank will too."

Nadine got up and went over to the shelf by the stereo. When she came back she dropped a tobacco pouch and a packet of Rizlas into Peter's lap. "Another one of Peter's many skills," she said. Then she sat on the arm of Peter's chair and started to hum.

Peter rolled two cigarettes and handed one to Frank. "Peace pipe," he said. "Kind of." He lit the other one and took a slow drag before passing it across to Nadine who now sat on the chair opposite with her legs curled up beneath her. She smiled at Peter and closed her eyes.

After his fifth or sixth drag Frank realised that the cigarette he was smoking wasn't having any effect at all. He held it to his nose. It smelt just like an ordinary cigarette. Peter was bending down, whispering something to Nadine. She smiled and opened her eyes and looked over at Frank.

"Well, Frank, what do you think?" Peter said.

"Fine," Frank said, sitting back in his chair.

"Start of a great adventure," Peter said, grinning.

Frank took another drag. Nadine was watching him now, though her eyes were like slits, and Peter was staring into the fire. He could smell the drug in the room and he remembered the wave of calm that rippled through his body that night in the cinema. He shut his eyes but it made no difference.

Peter stood in front of the fireplace with both hands shoved deep in the back pockets of his jeans. "I know," he said. "We'll play a game."

"Oh, lay off, Peter," Nadine said, her eyes still shut.

Peter was looking at Frank. "Charades," he said.

"Peter, no way," Nadine said. She drew her legs up tighter and rested her head on her knees.

"Listen," Peter said. "I have it. We all describe someplace we've never been. It could be any place. It could be real or out of your head. That doesn't matter. What's important is that you convince everyone else it exists. Then everyone asks questions and you have to answer them as best you can. And even if it's imagination you can't tell lies. Does that make sense, folks?"

"Sure, Peter," Nadine said. "Whatever you say." She shifted her weight in the chair.

"Come on, Nadine," Peter said. He reached for her arm but she pulled it tight against her side.

"Fug off," she said.

Peter waved the half-smoked joint in front of Nadine's nose. "No more big bad cigarettes for Nadine if Nadine doesn't play."

Nadine opened her eyes, shut them quickly, then opened them again. "Oh, all right," she said, reaching lazily for the joint. "Just for as long as this lasts."

Peter winked at Frank. "Right," he said. "Frank'll start."

"Yeah," said Nadine. "Peter's a bastard, but guests first, anyway."

Peter turned off the light and sat down on the floor beside Nadine's chair.

"Now, Frank," Nadine said. "Go on."

"I'm not sure what I'm supposed to do," Frank said.

"It's dead easy," Peter said. "OK, I'll try something just to get us started." He closed his eyes.

"It's all very, very serious," Nadine said, grinning at Frank.

"Nadine, shut up," Peter snapped.

Nadine stuck out her tongue and reached over and took the joint from his hand.

Peter said, "Now, listen. I see a white ocean and a blue mountain. Actually, there are loads of mountains and they're all blue and they seem to go on for ever and ever."

"And ever," Nadine yawned, loudly.

"Be quiet," Peter said.

"Question," Nadine said. She was leaning over the arm of the chair, the joint held loosely between her fingers. "What kind of blue are these mountains, anyway?"

"Jesus, I don't know," Peter said. "They're just your ordinary blue."

"I mean, are they sapphire-blue, or turquoise-blue, or indigo-blue, or what kind of fucking blue?"

"You tell me, Nadine. Whatever blue you want."

"No. You tell me. You're the one who started it."

"For fuck's sake, Nadine." Peter stood up and went over to the fireplace. "Just shut up."

Nadine looked over at Frank. "Maybe you can help us," she said.

Peter had turned his back and was staring into the fire.

"Go on," Nadine said to Frank. "Don't mind him."

Frank waited and it seemed like he would never say a word.

"Go on," Nadine said again. She had raised her voice.

"Sometimes, nothing ever prepares you for what people will do," Frank said. "Sometimes, I just wonder, that's all." This was how he started but he didn't know how he would tell the story or if the words would make any sense.

Peter and Nadine were both looking at him now. "What's the story, Frank?" Peter said, starting to laugh.

"Ssshh," Nadine said. "Shut up, you."

Frank looked at Nadine, and then at Peter. They each seemed younger than he had realised. They sat before him like children, their faces lit by the pale flames.

Then he heard his voice begin again. "Once," he said, "I had a son."

Of Course You Were

The clear skies and bright morning sunshine had promised another day of Indian summer, but on her way back to the office after lunch, Kate noticed the first idle clouds drifting in from the west. Now, as she sat in the restaurant with her mother, the city seemed to be cowering under a canopy of grey. Her mother, however, had chosen to ignore the change.

"Darling," she was saying, "you look so pale. What have you been at during all this glorious weather?"

"I have to work, you know, Mother," Kate said. "I can't afford to be a lady of leisure."

"You know, I've never really agreed with working wives."

"You never had to. Dad was loaded."

"He may have earned good money, but he most certainly was not loaded, as you say. Anyway, it was the principle of the thing. He wouldn't hear tell of it."

"Well, things are different now."

"Perhaps, but maybe you'll see it all in another light when you have children."

Kate picked up the menu and opened it.

"How is David, anyway?" her mother asked.

"Fine," Kate said.

"You should have brought him along. He's always so full of charm."

Kate broke a toasted bread stick in two and began to chew on a piece.

"Sometimes, you know, a woman can take her husband's qualities for granted. And vice versa, I might add."

Kate looked up from the menu. "I'm starving," she said. "Isn't it time we ordered."

Her mother put on her reading glasses and studied the menu.

"Well, I'm having the mozzarella salad and then the salmon. You should have the fish too, darling. It will do you good."

"Mother, you know I've always hated fish," Kate said.

When she finally caught the attention of a young waiter who was lounging by the doorway, Kate ordered carrot soup and chicken-liver pasta. As he took their order the waiter, who spoke with an American accent, smiled a lot, showing his brilliant white teeth.

"Oh, and of course we must have some wine," Kate's mother said and she ordered a bottle of house white.

When the waiter had left their table Kate's mother said, "Gosh, isn't he good-looking. He reminds me of one of those tennis players on TV. I bet he has those long tanned muscular legs."

"Oh, Mother," Kate said.

Across the street a busker gave a few quick strums on his guitar and started to sing 'Send Me the Pillow That You Dream On' in a loud, plaintive voice.

"Great," Kate said. "A singing comedian."

A couple came in and were seated at a nearby table.

Kate's mother said, in a low voice, "Do you see that pair? I'll bet you anything she's his mistress."

"What makes you say that?" Kate asked.

"I would think it's obvious, darling. She isn't wearing any wedding ring. And she's about half his age."

Kate glanced over at the couple. The man, whose hair was streaked with grey, was wearing a dark double-breasted suit. The woman wore a short cream linen dress. Every now and then she shook her long black hair away from her face.

"Mother," Kate said, "I wish you wouldn't make such superficial judgements about people."

"You should learn to relax, darling. Why don't you try yoga or something?"

"Please, give me a break."

"All right, but I worry about you sometimes."

"Don't bother," Kate said. "I can look after myself."

"Of course you can," her mother said.

When Kate looked at the couple again, she saw the woman dipping her little finger in her soup and then sticking it in her partner's mouth.

After coffee Kate lit a cigarette.

"I thought this was a no-smoking area," her mother said.

"Really?" Kate said. "I didn't notice."

"You really should give them up. Promise me you'll try."

"You know I can't promise something like that."

"I do wish you'd try. It's for your own good."

Kate took another drag on the cigarette.

"If only you were more resolute," her mother said.

"What do you mean by that, Mother?"

"You know what I mean."

"No, I don't," Kate said.

"Sticking at things is what I mean. Making up your mind about something and then carrying it through. That's what I mean."

"OK," Kate said. "No need to jump down my throat. Of course I know what resolute means."

"Forget it," her mother said, "I give up."

Kate said something in French but her mother ignored it.

Neither of them spoke for a while. Kate continued to smoke. Her mother's gaze wandered from table to table and, now and then, she took a quick sip of wine.

It seemed like a long time since Kate had last used her French. When she was a child her father decided, for the benefit of her education, that on one day every week he would speak to her only in French. She enjoyed it at first. It was a novelty trying to pronounce those delicate-sounding words and, after some time, she could put sentences together quite easily. And when, in secondary school, she took French as a subject she found she had an advantage over her classmates. She also realised that her father's pronunciation was far from perfect and so, during her early teens, she felt embarrassed by the whole thing and, whenever her father spoke to her in French, especially in public, she would reply in English. Later on, though, she discovered its usefulness when trying to get around her father. For example, if she wanted money, or if she was looking for permission to go to a disco or a party, French always seemed to work. Kate's mother would listen in silent frustration to these secret exchanges, but she never made any attempt to learn the language. Two years ago, when Kate visited her father in hospital for the last time, she thought he said something to her in French. But she was not sure. He had had a second stroke the night before and his words were faint and garbled.

Outside now the street lights were flickering on one by one and the busker, who had stopped singing, was rolling a cigarette.

When Kate looked at her watch again it was a quarter-past-eight. She excused herself and went down the spiral stairway near the back of the restaurant. She found a phone booth at the end of a narrow corridor. She dialled her home number. There was no reply, but she waited until the ringing tone had stopped.

In the Ladies she stood in front of the mirror and ran her fingers carefully through her hair, checking for signs of grey. She gave her teeth a quick brush and put on some fresh lipstick. Then she blew slowly on the glass, watching as her image fogged up and finally disappeared.

Upstairs, her mother was saying something to the young American waiter who had filled both glasses from a freshly opened bottle.

"Oh, Mother," Kate said, "don't you think we've had enough."

"Shush," her mother said. "You can never have enough of a good thing." She looked at the waiter. "Isn't that right, young man?"

The waiter smiled and said, "I guess so, ma'am."

"Please, we'll have less of the madam business."

"Oh, I am sorry," the waiter said, tugging at his serving napkin.

"It's perfectly all right. Just as long as you remember the next time."

Her mother winked at Kate and raised her glass to her lips.

"Oh, Mother, you shouldn't give him such a hard time," Kate said when the waiter had hurried to clear a recently vacated table.

"Nonsense," her mother said. "I'll leave him a nice tip. And, anyway, they enjoy it."

The next time Kate reached for the wine bottle she realised it was almost empty.

Up until quite recently Kate had never seen her mother take a drink, but she knew that at one stage in her life her mother had been a drinker. She knew this because of something she had overheard one night years ago when some visiting relatives had left after dinner. During the meal an aunt, one of her mother's many sisters, had brought up the story of Kate's fall. It was a story Kate had heard many times. It had become a family legend of sorts. According to the story, one summer afternoon, eighteen-month-old Kate (who was very adventurous) had crawled out of the window of an upstairs bedroom and fallen almost six feet onto the roof of the kitchen. She had escaped uninjured, apart from a few bruises and a gash over her left eye (the scar from which Kate still bore). Whenever this story was told her mother would laugh and say, "Yes, isn't she the miracle girl" and, inevitably, someone would pat Kate on the head and say, "the little rascal". What everyone always found highly amusing was the vision of Kate peering calmly over the edge of the roof at her hysterical mother down below, while her father rushed next door to borrow a ladder.

After this particular dinner, Kate had been put to bed and her parents were busy washing up in the kitchen. Kate decided to sneak down to the dining room for some left-over chocolates. As she reached the bottom of the stairs she heard her father say, "I wish you wouldn't wallow so much in that bloody story about the kid's accident. You know it would never have happened if you hadn't been drunk out of your skull." Kate waited for her mother's reply but she heard nothing but the clatter of dishes being rinsed and stacked.

Kate was ten at the time, and for years afterwards she lived in dread of the reckless creature that could be unleashed if her mother ever drank again.

Kate was watching the American waiter weaving between tables when she heard her mother saying, "Anyway, while you were away dolling yourself up in the loo, I noticed a man staring over in this direction."

"Really?" Kate said and she turned to take a quick look.

"Oh, don't bother now. He left a few minutes ago."

"What was he like? Was he rich and handsome?"

"You wouldn't believe me, of course. Well, let me tell you when I was your age, and quite a bit older even, I had plenty of admirers." She glanced quickly towards the window, trying to catch her reflection in the glass.

"I suppose I gave your father a hard time. And I wouldn't mind but he was so jealous. It used to drive him up the walls."

"Mother, believe me, most men are jealous."

"Not like your father was. With him it was almost like an obsession of some kind."

"How do you mean?"

"When your father and I were first married, we had quite a hectic social life. There were parties in our house every second weekend, or so it seemed. And, if not, there was always a party somewhere else. Some of these were business-related do's, but mostly they were with friends of ours. There was a lot of drinking done. Everything was always very civilised though. We had great times. But by degrees I began to notice your father's jealous streak."

"Like what?" Kate said.

"Well, I'd be talking to some man or other and your father would interrupt with some silly excuse, or he'd suggest that I mix more with the other guests. A few times on the way home from someone's house he asked me had I not noticed so and so's wife giving me dirty looks all night. I didn't give a curse about so and so's wife. It was ridiculous. I could be a bit of a flirt, I suppose, but there was never anything to it. I was just being friendly. But after a while these parties became more of an ordeal than anything else. I felt he was watching me the whole time. Should I speak to that person? Did I smile too often at somebody? Had I been over-enthusiastic in greeting this or that man? I felt I could hardly talk to anyone. My self-confidence was being affected. I actually refused to go to a few parties. Then he'd say it would be bad for business not to turn up. The whole thing became unbearable. I know it might sound strange, but I think I would have left him if I hadn't ended up in hospital."

"Mother, what are you talking about?"

Her mother reached across and took Kate's hand in hers.

"It's got really nothing to do with you. And it was such a long time ago. You weren't even born."

"Mother. Please. Tell me."

"It's not a nice story, by any means."

She stopped for a moment and looked out the window. The busker had gathered up his coins and was packing his guitar away. From somewhere down the street came the exotic beat of salsa music.

"In those days, darling, the business was just getting off the ground and your father worked very long hours. So, during the week I was left to my own devices for most of the time. I used to read a lot and in the evenings I'd go for long walks in the park. I'd walk for miles. I think I must have known every nook and cranny in the place. Anyway, one spring evening, while I was out walking, this huge bunch of roses arrived in the porch. For me. Totally out of the blue and without any sender's name. Your father got home in the meantime and when I came in, I saw the flowers thrown there on the table. He was furious. He started asking me all these questions. Where was I all day? What was I doing coming in at this hour? I could smell drink off him too. I was really frightened. He accused me of this, that and the other. It was awful. I began to cry and then I started screaming and he punched me in the stomach. I fell backwards and knocked against the table. The next thing I was in the emergency ward of the hospital."

She stopped and looked at Kate. "How did we end up talking about all this?"

"Oh God," Kate said. Her hand felt cold against her mother's skin. "How long were you in hospital?"

"A while, darling. You see it was more complicated than you think. I was almost two months pregnant at the time."

"Oh, no," Kate said, "what happened to the baby?"

"I don't remember very much about the hospital. Everything happened in a kind of haze. Afterwards a nurse tried to explain it to me. She said it was like having a very heavy period. I will always remember the way she said that."

Kate touched her mother's cheek.

"What did Dad do? What did he say?"

"I never told him. He never knew a thing about it."

"How could he not know? Surely he must have realised something."

"Men don't notice those things, I suppose. And, anyway, while I was in hospital he had to go abroad on business for a few days."

"You mean you never told him anything?"

"I wanted to tell him and then it was too late. There wasn't any point anymore."

She took a drink of water and said, as if to herself, "Afterwards we came to a sort of unspoken arrangement. He went wherever he wished and if I wanted to go to a party I went."

She looked at Kate and smiled. "And then, darling, we had you."

She was about to say something else when the sound of falling rain filled the room. At every table people seemed to have stopped talking. On the street passersby ran for shelter. A waiter rushed outside to unfurl an awning over the abandoned tables near the doorway.

"Won't it be wonderful to smell the rain again," Kate's mother said. "This unseasonable weather makes people restless. Everything will be back to its old self tomorrow."

It grew suddenly cool in the restaurant and Kate wished she had brought a jacket.

"I'm tired," her mother said. "I think we should be going home."

Kate called for the bill and when she was paying she asked the cashier to phone for a taxi.

They were driving through the suburbs. Kate was staring out at the reflection of wet light on the pavement.

"Darling," her mother said and Kate turned towards her. "Do you think we were happy, your father and I? In the end, I mean."

"Yes," Kate said. "Of course you were."

Neither of them spoke for a while.

Then Kate said, "Mother, who was it who sent you the flowers that time?" Her mother looked at her. In the dim glow of the cab Kate could see the brilliant blue of her eyes.

"How could I remember that? It was such a long time ago."

Then she laughed. "Don't look at me like that, darling. It's perfectly harmless for someone to send you flowers, you know."

As they turned a corner her mother leaned closer and put her arm around Kate's shoulder. "Darling, you looked so beautiful tonight. You know I'll always be proud of you, no matter what."

They fell silent again and all that could be heard was the sound of the windscreen wipers slapping back and forth. Then the taxi driver began to tell them a story about a fare he had picked up outside a club on Leeson Street the other night.

Meeting The Muse

Her name was Beatrice and she had once been regarded as the most beautiful woman in Dublin, but in the beginning Stuart and Caroline knew nothing about this. Stuart first saw her during the interval one opening night at the theatre. Actually, it was Caroline who drew his attention to the woman with the hat.

"Look at that hat," Caroline said. "Can you imagine having to sit behind that all night?"

Stuart looked and saw a woman sitting in a corner of the foyer. She was wearing a long black dress and a large black hat with a mass of black feathers around the brim. She sat alone, leafing through the theatre programme, stopping now and then to take a sip from a cup on the table beside her.

"What age do you think she is?" Caroline asked.

"Sixty. Seventy, maybe," Stuart ventured.

"Eighty, at least," Caroline said. "Look at her. She could have walked straight out of the 1930s. That dress would be worth a fortune in the antique clothes' trade."

Just then, the theatre manager, on his way through the crowd, stopped to say a few words to the woman.

"I wonder who she is," Caroline said. "I'm sure she's someone I should know from somewhere."

Stuart looked at the woman again. She sat with her head held erect, her face almost hidden in the shadow of the large hat. She seemed preoccupied and completely alone. Then the bell rang and she disappeared from view as everyone returned to the theatre for the start of the second act.

Stuart had begun to lose interest in the play— a modern adaptation of Chekhov full of boredom and silence — when a slight commotion started in some seats close to the stage. Voices were raised and suddenly the woman with the hat stood up and made her way to the end of her row.

"There goes her ladyship, daft as a brush, probably," Caroline whispered as they watched the woman walk towards the exit.

One evening, a few weeks later while she was making dinner, Caroline said, "I was in Brown Thomas' at lunchtime and guess who I saw."

Stuart had no idea.

"The woman at the play. The one with the hat. Remember, she walked out."

"Are you sure?" Stuart asked.

"It would be difficult to mistake her. She was wearing another beautiful old hat and one of those ancient coats with a fox collar. She came in looking for rouge. 'You mean blusher,' the assistant said. Her ladyship goes: 'I mean exactly what I say. Rouge, blusher, you may call it what you like.' She has one of those accents. She might have been an actor, once upon a time."

The next evening, on her way home from work, Caroline saw the woman again — going down into the basement of a house in Pembroke Street, just around the corner from where she and Stuart lived.

At this time, Stuart and Caroline had been living together for almost two years in a flat on the top-floor of a house not far from Fitzwilliam Square.

Caroline worked as a copy-writer with an advertising agency. She was twenty-eight.

Stuart was an American, from Boston. Once, he had been a lecturer in nineteenth-century English literature in one of the smaller colleges in the Boston area. Now he was trying his hand at writing, full-time. He had come to Ireland shortly after his divorce from Jessica — a limber New Jersey girl with a tongue like a warm snake and a Masters in history from Princeton — whom he had married when they were both twenty-five.

Whenever Stuart thought about his old married life — which he did now with less and less frequency — he remembered best the summers at Jessica's family's holiday house on Nantucket when he would lock himself away all morning to write in an attic room that echoed with the sound of the ocean, while Jessica swam and played beach tennis with the Johnsons.

Mike and Laura Johnson — both teaching at Harvard Law School — had been friends of Jessica's since college. Both couples had married in the same year. Stuart and Jessica, and Mike and Laura spent four weeks together each summer during the first years of their marriage, and things might have continued in that manner except that in the third summer Stuart fell in love with Laura Johnson.

It began during a long walk on the beach when Laura told Stuart all about Mike's infidelities. Back in Boston, the following winter, they would meet to talk, and finally they started sleeping together.

When Mike — himself an expert on deception — found out, he told Jessica. After that, things could never be the same again.

Laura and Mike stayed together. Laura said that she had come to realise the whole thing had been her way of getting back at Mike, and now that they were even, she hoped they would have more respect for each other.

Stuart tried to patch things up with Jessica, but in the end she said she wasn't prepared to wait around until the next Laura Johnson came along to sweep him off his feet.

After the divorce, Stuart was unhappy and restless. He needed a change of scenery. Someone suggested that he go to Ireland for a while. It seemed like a good idea. Having lived in Boston all his life, Stuart looked upon Ireland as not an entirely foreign country, but it would be different, and people were always telling him how beautiful and friendly it was.

So he quit his job, and late that fall, he left for Ireland. He hadn't had much time for writing in the past while; now he was going to start again. With his share of the money from the sale of the house he reckoned he had enough to get by on for a few years.

He spent the first two months in a house near the Burren, recommended to him by a friend of a friend. The roof leaked, and it took him the best part of each morning to get warm after struggling to light the back-burner with damp turf in the large old-fashioned kitchen.

He bought a second-hand bike and twice a week he would set off for the nearby village to do the shopping. The elderly men and women he got chatting to in the shop and post office and in the local pub were invariably curious. They would ask if he had ever come across any of their relations in Boston, and what had brought him to County Clare and then — inevitably — was he married?

He was starting to feel homesick, and as he was not getting much writing done, he decided to move to Dublin — a city with a strong literary tradition where he would at least find it easier to keep dry and warm.

In Dublin he rented a flat off the North Circular Road and set himself a strict routine of work. He knew nobody in the city and at night he would find himself being drawn to the pubs, especially the older ones near St Stephen's Green.

One Friday — after another frustrating morning spent working — he went to the pub early. He wanted to get drunk, but instead he met Caroline. The after-work drinkers had not yet arrived and he noticed her sitting just inside the door of the snug. She was reading a book of John Updike stories, and Stuart watched her from his place at the bar counter, her eyes moving quickly over the pages as she read, her auburn hair turning copper in the evening light that flooded through the large window above her head.

Stuart hadn't read anything by John Updike since his student days, but Jessica had been a big fan. She had read practically everything. She called him "The Master." Once, after things had begun to go wrong, he overheard Jessica saying during a phone conversation with her sister, "I think I finally know how the characters in a John Updike story must feel."

Eventually Caroline put her book aside and took out a cigarette. She began searching in her bag for matches and when she didn't find any she came up to the counter and asked Stuart for a light.

They started talking. He asked her what she thought of the story she had been reading.

"The characters seem so pathetic and confused. Are all Americans like that?" she asked.

"No," Stuart said. "Only sometimes, maybe."

Six months later, when Caroline's flat mate got a job in London, Stuart moved into the flat in Fitzwilliam Place. It was bright and spacious, with a view of the canal from one window and though it faced eastwards, in the evenings the reflective metal panels of a tall office building across the way filled the living-room with the captured light of the setting sun.

Stuart knew it was a place where he could write. He began work on a novel. When the novel wasn't going well, he wrote short stories. If the stories didn't sell he wrote articles with an Irish flavour for some small publications in America. Sometimes, Toni, an editor with one of the Sunday newspapers and a friend of Caroline's, would ring and ask him to do a piece. Of course he didn't make a lot of money from any of this, though the newspaper articles paid much better than the stories. Caroline still looked after the rent while they both waited for the day when Stuart would sell a story to *The New Yorker,* or else make enough progress with his novel to enable him to earn a large advance from some prestigious English publisher.

Sometimes, Stuart fled the flat and got on a bus and travelled around the city, watching people from the upper deck. On the worst days, when the words wouldn't come at all, he would go to bed in the afternoon. Caroline would come home and find him there — crumpled, empty and silent. Then she would call in to Shane who lived in the flat across the landing and get some grass and the three of them would smoke and talk and listen to music until the early hours.

Occasionally, Stuart would go drinking with Denis, a civil servant he had met at a poetry reading. The first thing that had struck him about Denis was his strong resemblance to Brendan Behan. There he was, canny and alert, standing by the free drinks table after the reading, in his dark suit, with his tie loosened and a full bottle of wine in his hand.

He offered to refill Stuart's glass. "When is the EC going to bring in some sort of set-aside scheme for poetry, I wonder?" he asked.

Stuart was confused.

"Some way of paying these fellows for every poem they don't write, like the farmers are paid for not sowing certain crops."

Denis turned up regularly at readings and launches. "I've learnt from experience that the only sane reason for going to these things is the free booze." He gave the impression that he knew everyone involved in the literary scene and he moved from pub to pub around the city, talking and gathering stories. He would point out some elderly gentleman sipping a pint in a corner of the Arts Club bar "I could tell you a thing or two about your man," he'd say. Dublin was still full of characters, according to Denis. "Just as much as in Joyce's time, and don't let anyone try to convince you otherwise."

Stuart knew very little about Denis, apart from the fact that he was married, had two children and lived somewhere on the northside. Whenever they met they talked almost exclusively about literary matters. Denis read all the reviews and he had a poor opinion of all current fiction. He was always the first with news about who had recently changed publishers and who had been offered the biggest advances, and he knew who was likely to receive bursaries from the Arts Council. He would regularly warn Stuart of the dangers of selling his soul to Mammon. Stuart found most of this talk depressing, but whenever he relayed any of it to Caroline, she would laugh and say, "You know you shouldn't believe anything he says. He sounds like an absolute fucking chancer."

Summer came. In June there was a spell of unusually hot weather. Stuart could not work. Each morning he would go to the park and read, or write in his journal. Sometimes, he would do nothing but smoke and stare up into the cloudless sky and hope for inspiration.

When he was lucky he would have the makings of a joint from Shane, and when lunchtime came and the park filled with workers from the surrounding offices, he would lie in the shade and watch the girls and think of the seventies back in Boston and afternoons spent on the Common, waiting for some shining long-legged beauty to arrive fresh from her parents' blue-tiled pool.

Later, when the office workers had finally drifted away, the gardener would resume his work — dragging a roller across the tennis courts or nonchalantly clipping the grass along the edges of the gravel paths — and later still some tennis players might arrive or, sometimes, a group from the Arts Club would come to play croquet in the quivering heat of the afternoon.

On one of these afternoons, Stuart was watching a couple playing tennis. They were good players, but after some time he became drowsy watching the constant back and forth motion of the ball. He closed his eyes and fell asleep.

When he woke, the tennis players were gone. The park was deserted apart from a woman in a sunhat who sat reading on a bench beneath a large sycamore tree. Stuart no longer bothered wearing a watch, but he had arranged to meet Caroline for a drink after work and he didn't want to be late again. He gathered up his things and went over to the woman on the bench. As he got closer, she looked up from her reading and he realised she was the same woman he had seen months earlier at the theatre — the woman Caroline had dubbed Madame Rouge. She was wearing a white summer dress and white shoes and stuck in the band of her faded straw hat was a pale yellow rose.

Stuart asked her the time. It was a quarter-past-five, she told him. He thanked her and was about to go when she said, "You're lucky, you know, that you were in the shade all this time. People nowadays are so foolish when it comes to the sun."

Yes, Stuart agreed, they often were.

She could never stand much of the sun herself, she said. "Many years ago I was staying with friends of mine in the south of France. They were sailing fanatics and every morning at the crack of dawn we would take off in their yacht and as the day got hotter and hotter I would eventually have to go below deck and lie down and every so often sprinkle pieces of crushed ice on my skin. There was never any ice left over for drinks afterwards." She laughed. "It was the most uncomfortable holiday of my entire life."

The sun — which had already begun its slow descent above the houses on the far side of the square — was shining into her eyes, making her squint as she looked up at him. "I do wish you'd sit down," she said. "It would be much easier for me to see you."

As Stuart was sitting down on the bench, the magazine she had been reading fell to the ground. He picked it up; it was a battered and creased copy of *Vogue*.

"Oh," she said, slipping it back into a small carrier bag. "I like to keep up with these things."

She looked at him again. "You're an American," she said.

"Yes," Stuart said, laughing.

She smiled. "Of course I recognised the accent, but you have that American way about you, too. That looseness of limbs, that swagger, I think they call it. I noticed it as you were walking across the court."

"Really?" Stuart said. "I'd hope it wasn't so obvious."

"But why not? Why on earth would you want to hide that? I remember the first real Americans we saw in this part of the world — GIs who came to study in Trinity after the war. They were fine-looking men — people would stop in the street just to look at them.

"And then when President Kennedy came over in 1963. Now that was an extraordinary sight. John Fitzgerald and Jacqueline Bouvier Kennedy — the two of them together, being driven through the streets of Dublin. You have no idea, I'm sure. People here had never seen anything like it before. Half the women in the country would have thrown themselves at his feet."

She laughed, ruefully. "All that rubbish that's come out about Kennedy recently, the stories in the newspapers. Do you believe it? Does anyone in America really believe it?"

Stuart said that unfortunately there seemed to be a good basis for many of the stories.

"Oh, no," she said. "But people are like that, aren't they. They will always try to drag down the great and the beautiful." She reached up to adjust her sunhat and a few strands of long grey hair fell down about her face. "Oh, dear, my hair. It's a job," she said, tucking it back underneath the hat. "Anyway, it's getting a bit chilly for me. I should be making my way back home."

As they parted, they exchanged first names and Stuart said he would probably see her in the park again.

"Certainly," she said. "I do hope so."

Caroline had already been waiting outside the Pembroke Bar for half-an-hour when Stuart arrived. She was sitting at a table near the doorway, looking brown and indolent.

She glanced at him and then at her watch. "My, my," she said. "Who have we here?"

Stuart apologised and ordered two drinks. He told Caroline that he had been talking to the woman with the hat.

"So, what did you find out about her?" Caroline asked, peering at him over the top of her sunglasses.

Stuart said he had managed to find out very little except that her first name was Beatrice.

"Beatrice," Caroline said. "Wasn't that the name of the woman Dante was in love with?"

"Dante?" Stuart asked.

"Dante Al-something or other, the Italian poet from the Middle Ages. Don't tell me you've never heard of him. A friend of mine did Italian in college and she was always reading these books on Dante and Dante's *Inferno*."

"Oh, that Dante," Stuart said.

"Yes, Stuart, that Dante. Which one did you have in mind?" She turned to wave as Shane, their neighbour, drove past in his white MG. The roof was rolled back and Stuart caught a glimpse of a girl with long dark hair sitting in the passenger seat.

"That reminds me," Caroline said. "Maybe you should cut down on the old funny cigarettes. They could be fucking up your memory."

Stuart looked at her. She laughed and sat back in her chair. The sun hovered in a gap between the houses across the street. The glass Caroline was raising to her lips flung splashes of sunlight onto her freckled skin. "What else did she have to say for herself anyway, the mad old woman?" she asked.

The following week Stuart met Beatrice in the park again. She was sitting on the same bench, wearing the same dress and sunhat, watching a game of doubles on a nearby court.

He sat down beside her.

"Do you play?" she asked.

"Not much," he said.

"Oh, you should," she said. "It's important for young people to keep active. I remember one glorious summer in England. All we seemed to do was get up each morning, put on our tennis whites and go to the courts. We'd play until lunchtime when someone would arrive with a picnic hamper and we would stop for a few hours. Then in the cool of the evening, the games would start again. There were ten or twelve of us, young men and women, all in our twenties then. Some even ended up marrying their tennis partners."

She talked about England for another while and then about
her life in the South of France — in Juan les Pins and
Villefranche — in the old days, and about trips across the
Mediterranean to Morocco and Algiers.

Her blue eyes sparkled as she spoke. Her voice was crisp
and clear — each word pronounced distinctly, her tongue
lingering over certain vowels.

Each time they met during that summer, Beatrice would
tell Stuart stories about her life abroad. He liked to listen to
them, though sometimes he would lose track as her memories
wandered from one country to another. All of the stories were
vivid and full of detail, but now and then Stuart found himself
doubting the veracity of what he was hearing. Whenever he
attempted to ask her questions about her personal life she
would deftly avoid giving away any information. In the end
he realised he knew very little about Beatrice, except that she
seemed to have once led a good life and travelled quite a bit.

Around this time Toni offered Caroline and Stuart tickets for
another opening night. Stuart arrived at the theatre shortly
before curtain-up. Caroline and Toni were already there; he
could see them standing at the bar, as he made his way across
the crowded foyer.

Toni — tall and skinny, with her hair cropped and sleek —
had a gin and tonic raised to her lips. She reminded Stuart of
one of those girls in *The Great Gatsby* who kept turning up at
parties. She was listening to something Caroline was telling
her, all the while letting her gaze wander slowly over the
crowd.

She had just spotted Stuart and had begun waving to him
when someone in the crowd grabbed his arm. He turned and

saw Beatrice. She was dressed exactly as she had been on that first night.

"Please, I'd like you to meet someone," she said, and she led him to a table by the window. "This is my granddaughter, Alannah, from San Francisco," she said, introducing Stuart to a striking girl with lightly tanned skin and long blonde hair.

"Alannah is over here for a few months, touring around. Maybe, as a fellow American, you could give her some advice."

Stuart said he'd love to sometime, but before they could make arrangements a voice came over the intercom asking people to please take their seats. Stuart excused himself, saying he would see them during the interval.

Caroline and Toni were still at the bar.

"Well, hi," Toni said, leaning forward slightly, allowing him to kiss her briefly on the cheek. "I saw you," she said. "Disappearing off like that with the Black Widow. What are you up to? I think we should be told."

Stuart laughed and looked at Caroline. "It was Beatrice," he said, by way of explanation.

"She's a friend of Stuart's," Caroline said, grinning at Toni, "someone he meets in the park."

"Oh," Toni said, "you know Beatrice Cunningham. Now I'm interested." She leaned closer to Stuart. "Tell me more."

"Do you know her?" Caroline asked.

"Well, I know of her. Vaguely. She's one of those people you always see at things. But not everyone is on speaking terms with her."

She smiled at Stuart and raised another gin and tonic to her lips. "I think she had something to do with that poet, a long time ago now, obviously."

Caroline mentioned the name of a well-known poet who had been dead for many years.

"That's him," Toni said, gleefully. She lowered her voice. "I think there was some kind of scandal."

As she was speaking it was announced that the curtain would be going up in three minutes.

"Oh, it's opening night, for God's sake," Toni said, reaching for her glass again. "What's the bloody rush?" She swallowed the last of her gin and tonic before following Stuart and Caroline into the auditorium.

At the interval Toni declared the play atrocious, and rather than return for the second act she persuaded Caroline and Stuart to join her for a drink.

"I wonder," Toni said to Stuart while Caroline was ordering drinks, "could I entice you to do a piece for us on that lady friend of yours, Beatrice Cunningham. I'm sure there's oodles of interesting stuff there, and you seem to be one of the favoured."

Stuart said he didn't think so.

"Well, think about it. And let me know when you've changed your mind."

The next time he met Beatrice in the park, Stuart apologised for having missed her and her granddaughter that night at the theatre.

"It doesn't matter," Beatrice said. "She's well able to look after herself." Alannah had hired a car and gone down the country for a month, she explained. Perhaps he'd meet her when she got back.

She asked him then what he thought of Alannah.

"Oh, she's beautiful," Stuart said.

"Yes," Beatrice said, smiling to herself. "So they say."

Stuart found the photograph in an out-of-print biography of the poet in the basement of Fred Hanna's bookshop. It had been taken on an outing to the Dublin mountains sometime in the mid-1930s. There was a group of nine or ten people altogether, but no names were given apart from those of the poet and another well-known writer of the period. Easily identifiable, in the middle of the group was the poet, his hat pushed back rakishly on his head, a cigarette in his hand. Beside him stood a tall young woman with long fair hair. She had an arm draped casually around the poet's shoulder and she was looking straight out towards the camera. Her gaze was steady and confident and she was smiling. The day must have been windy. The other women in the photograph had neat shoulder-length hair or dark beret-style hats, but the young woman's hair was loose and she was using her right hand to keep it from blowing across her face.

Stuart had no doubt who the young woman was. She looked uncannily like Alannah. He checked the index for Beatrice's name, then read quickly through some pages, but could find no mention of her. He would have bought the book but it was a first-edition hardback and he could not afford it.

When he told Caroline about the photograph, she said, "And now she's ended up this odd creature. Isn't that frightening?"

Stuart said he wouldn't call her odd.

"OK, well eccentric, then. She's definitely eccentric, by anybody's standards."

Stuart mentioned Beatrice's name, and her connection with the poet, to Denis the next time they met. Denis had never heard of her, but he said he'd ask Mr O'Shaughnessy — a retired Civil Servant from his department. "O'Shaughnessy knows about every camp-follower and hanger-on there ever was."

Stuart said he was sure Beatrice had been more than a camp-follower.

"We shall see," Denis said.

Some weeks later, Denis arranged for Stuart to meet Mr O'Shaughnessy in the Arts Club. "This is the man who'll be able to tell you all you need to know about your friend, the Muse."

"Stuart is a Yank," Denis told Mr O'Shaughnessy. "He's interested in that kind of thing."

"Well," Mr O'Shaughnessy said, "if it's Beatrice Cunningham you're talking about, it must be well over ten years since I last saw her. She was dining by herself in the old Royal Hibernian Hotel. I haven't set eyes on her since that night."

Mr O'Shaughnessy took a pipe from his pocket and began to light it. Denis raised his pint to his lips and winked at Stuart.

After taking a few sucks on his pipe, Mr O'Shaughnessy continued. "I don't know how they met or when, but it was an odd set-up, I can tell you. He was at least twenty years older than her, but he looked even older because of the drink, and the hard life, I suppose. You couldn't miss them on the street. They were quite a sight. She had this long blonde hair and she always wore it down. Now, back in those times women would cut their hair after a certain age, or else wear it up in a bun or whatever. You'd never see them wearing it down their backs out on the street. Well, Beatrice did. She didn't care. Not that she was ever strealish or anything. In fact, she was always well-turned-out.

"Anyway, you'd see the pair of them swanning around — especially during the Holy Hour, when the pubs were shut — she walking regally along and your man waddling beside her, throwing a look up at her every now and then." Mr O'Shaughnessy gave a short wheezy laugh and took a quick drink of whiskey.

"It could be quite funny sometimes. They'd have these horrific rows. You could hear them from one end of Grafton Street to the other. He'd be calling her a prostitute and a whore at the top of his voice, and all probably because she'd looked sideways at some young lad. And she'd be shouting back for all she was worth, saying he was nothing but a dirty old lecher. She was well able for him, I can tell you."

"Sounds charming," Denis said.

"Oh, charming is right," Mr O'Shaughnessy said. "But they were of no harm to anyone except themselves." He stopped to rekindle his pipe and Denis ordered another round.

Stuart sat back on the faded settee and watched Mr O'Shaughnessy carefully packing tobacco into the bowl of his pipe. His soft country accent and the smell of the pipe smoke reminded Stuart of the old men — first-generation Irish emigrants — who used to gather in groups of three and four in a park near Boston Harbour on summer evenings to talk and to watch the sun going down. He would pass them on his way home from baseball practice, the heft of the baseball bat between his fingers.

Mr O'Shaughnessy coughed before continuing. "Of course, you know all about the poem your man wrote about her. There was a rumour doing the rounds for a while that he had actually written it for another girl entirely, some American, but that's a load of nonsense. Beatrice Cunningham was the only person who could have inspired that poem. When it appeared in one of the papers it created a bit of a stir. Within months everyone seemed to know it. You'd hear it recited and sung in pubs and at parties and the like. You couldn't imagine it happening nowadays. His poor wife was scandalised."

He stopped for a moment, lost in thought. "It's a wonderful poem, no doubt about it. Marvellous." He quoted a few lines.

"I haven't seen her in years. She must be into her eighties by now, I suppose, but if either of you had seen her back then. I can tell you." Mr O'Shaughnessy smiled.

"After all that fuss about the poem, it seems it was he who finished things between them. It's strange, isn't it? People knowing about you like that, even pointing you out on the street. Your praises being sung, literally, all over the place and your man goes back to his wife. For a while, anyway. Of course the whole thing was hopeless from the start."

"What happened afterwards?" Stuart asked.

"Oh, she disappeared for years and years. The story was that she had married a rich Frenchman and was living in Paris. Then someone ran into her in London after the war. There were a lot of stories you wouldn't want to believe. Next thing, she was back in Dublin and she married a High Court judge on the q.t. He was a good bit older than she was. He died about twenty years ago and left her the house in Pembroke Street. I believe she couldn't afford the upkeep of a place like that and let most of it out in flats and offices."

It was getting late. Mr O'Shaughnessy finished his whiskey and glanced over at the clock behind the bar.

"Well there you have it. She came from a well-do-do family, horsy people in County Meath. She was studying at the university. No joke at the time. She gave it all up to traipse around after your man from pub to pub. You'd wonder what on earth made her do it."

"Yes," Denis said winking at Stuart again. "I suppose the moral of the story is that you're better off having nothing to do with poets and writers and the like."

"Maybe that's it," Mr O'Shaughnessy said, smiling. "Maybe you're right there, my friend." He stood up, put on his coat and hat and bade them goodnight.

Already it was autumn. Nobody went to the park any more. Soon the tennis nets would be taken down, and the faded white markings of the tennis courts would eventually be washed away by the rain.

Stuart hadn't seen Beatrice in weeks. Then, one afternoon, Toni rang. "Have you done anything about that Beatrice Cunningham piece?" she asked.

Stuart said he hadn't really thought about it since, and anyway he was busy.

Toni laughed. "Busy my bottom. Caroline tells me you sit around all day smoking shit and staring out the window. That isn't busy in my book."

Stuart told her he would think about it, but he already knew that Beatrice's story was too valuable to waste in a newspaper article.

Toni rang again the next day. "Listen, Stuart, I've been thinking about your piece. Why don't you take the Black Widow out to dinner. Somewhere nice, somewhere chic. And bring Caroline along. She'll get her talking in no time."

A month later, Stuart finally managed to arrange dinner with Beatrice. Caroline came too.

The restaurant was in South William Street. Beatrice seemed to be impressed. "You've certainly picked a nice place," she said, looking around admiringly at the large gilt-framed mirrors and the white ornate columns. She was wearing a long green dress and her hair as always was kept hidden, this time beneath a black cloche. Throughout the meal she wore a pair of black chiffon gloves.

Shortly before starters were served Beatrice excused herself and went out to the Ladies.

Caroline took a large gulp of wine and grinned. "Well, I'm enjoying this more than I expected," she said. "She's a bit scatty, but she's definitely what you might call entertaining."

Stuart topped up all three glasses with wine. "Do you think you could get her talking?"

Caroline laughed. "I don't think there's any problem there. She hasn't shut up since we've met."

"Not that kind of talk. I mean, talking about her past and all that."

"Oh, I see. The only thing of interest in her whole life is the time she spent as some dead poet's bit-on-the-side."

"I didn't say that."

Caroline drank more wine. "Toni seems to think the same thing, actually. Has she been on to you about doing a story?"

"No, she hasn't," Stuart said.

"I'm not sure if I believe you."

When Beatrice sat back in at the table, she started to question Caroline about the dress she was wearing, and all through the starter and main course Caroline and Beatrice talked about fashion.

They were now on their second bottle of wine. Stuart and Caroline were doing most of the drinking; Beatrice was too busy talking to take more than an occasional sip.

There was a lull in the conversation while they were waiting to order dessert.

Beatrice said, "Stuart, you've barely said a word all evening."

"He's feeling a bit left out," Caroline said, grinning across at Stuart. "I think he'd rather talk to you about life in Bohemian Dublin long ago."

"What do you mean?" Beatrice asked.

"Well," Caroline said, smiling, "Stuart thinks he knows who you are."

"Who I am?" Beatrice said and she laughed uneasily. "What on earth are you talking about?"

Stuart said, "She means we've heard that you moved in those circles, once upon a time."

Beatrice stared at him. There was a look of dread in her eyes. She raised a gloved hand to her cheek. "I've really no idea what either of you are talking about," she said. "I think you must have gotten me mixed up with somebody else."

She excused herself then, saying she was going to the Ladies.

Stuart glared over at Caroline. "Couldn't you have been a bit more subtle?"

Caroline laughed. "Actually, I think I was doing her a favour." She leaned across the table towards him. "I think she's an exceptionally nice lady. I don't think she deserves to have you trying to dig up the dirt on her past so that Toni can print the whole thing in her newspaper."

"I want it for myself, not for Toni. I know I could use it."

"That's pathetic."

"No, it's not. It's called gathering material."

"I thought you were supposed to make it up. I thought that was the whole idea."

Stuart shrugged. "Some things are better than anything you could ever make up."

He watched Beatrice walking slowly back to the table, her body stiff and erect.

"How strange," she said, as she was sitting down, "they have bottles of mineral water in the loo."

"I'm sorry," Stuart said. "We didn't mean to offend you."

"Never mind," Beatrice said. "Anyone can make a mistake." She smiled at Caroline. "Imagine thinking I was this other person. Obviously someone with a more interesting past than mine, whoever she is."

She laughed and looked at Stuart again. "Well, that's a good one."

They talked for a while then about which recent theatre productions they had and hadn't seen and, after finishing the last of the wine, agreed it was time to be going home.

Stuart and Caroline accompanied Beatrice back to the house in Pembroke Street.

"Well, I've had a really lovely night," Beatrice said. She kissed Caroline on the cheek. "I'm sure I'll see both of you again soon." She waved goodbye and went down the steps to the basement flat.

Stuart and Caroline walked on in silence for a short distance, Caroline slightly in front, her shoes making an annoying tapping sound on the footpath.

They were passing the park when Stuart said, "You know you really let me down tonight."

Caroline stopped and turned to face him. "OK, let's talk about letting people down so. Stuart, you don't need me to do that. You've made a very good job of it yourself. I mean, here you are, you're thirty-four years of age, you're supposed to be a writer — at least that's what I keep telling people — and the best you can do is try to get an unfortunate old woman to tell stories about her past so you can put it in a book."

"I don't see what the big deal is."

"Why can't you let her be? How would you like it if in fifty years time some nosey shit came snooping around, questioning me about our love life. Now, that would make an exciting story."

She walked on a few steps and stopped again. "Anyway, you needn't worry. Nobody's going to be that interested in finding out about you. Because you'll never be a good enough writer. You haven't got the guts or the talent for it."

She hurried on and crossed the street to the house where they lived. Stuart stood and watched as she climbed the steps and went inside.

He waited on the footpath for a short while, looking up at the house, until he saw the lights come on in the windows of the flat. Then he started walking. A light rain had begun to fall. When he reached Baggot Street, he turned in the direction of St Stephen's Green. A barman, standing in the doorway of Toners, bade him goodnight.

He was passing Doheny & Nesbitts when he heard an American voice ringing out. He followed it inside. The pub wasn't very full. He walked as far as the back bar, and was on his way out again, when he saw Beatrice's granddaughter. She was sitting on a stool at the bar between two young men in suits — businessmen probably — their briefcases abandoned on the floor nearby.

As he stood at the counter, waiting to be served, he noticed the girl resting her hand briefly on the knee of one of the men. She was telling them about something that had happened to her down in Cork. The young men were listening intently.

Stuart took a seat at one of the small tables along the wall. From there, he could observe them without being noticed. He could hear most of the conversation quite clearly.

Another round of drinks was ordered and one of the young men began to tell a story, but after a while Stuart lost interest in what he was saying. He had heard that kind of story before — the kind young Irish men told to young foreign women, especially young American women.

Alannah's long blonde hair glowed in the dim pub light and whenever she laughed she would throw back her head and let her hair fall away from her shoulders.

At one stage, Alannah went out to the Ladies, and on her way back Stuart was certain that she stared at him for a moment. But if she had recognised him, she did not let on as she returned to her companions at the bar.

Stuart ordered another pint. This was the first Dublin pub he had ever had a drink in. He had even got drunk here a few times.

It was here too, in the snug, that he had first seen Caroline. The pub was not a particular favourite of hers and he had not been there in a long time. He looked around at the faded signs, the mirrors advertising whiskeys no longer on the market, and at the low darkened ceiling — described in guidebooks as being stained by ancient cigarette smoke and the biting wit of brilliant Dublin raconteurs.

He heard Alannah laughing again. He wanted to speak to her, but what would he say? She had been in Ireland a few months, so he couldn't even ask her for news from home.

He was about to go up to the counter again, in the hope that he might catch her eye, when he saw her suddenly get up, put on her coat, kiss both men quickly on the cheek and leave.

He followed her out into the street. She had already hailed a taxi and was getting into the back seat. He was about to call out, "Wait, please, remember me," when the car door shut and the taxi disappeared in the traffic that was drifting out in the direction of Ballsbridge.

Stuart turned and began walking towards the Green. The rain had cleared. The streets and pavements were slowly drying. The night air was cool. He passed the entrance to the Shelbourne Hotel where, one night the previous Christmas, he had seen two women in fur coats, their faces pressed in curiosity against the darkened windows of a stretch limousine.

He continued on past the tall eighteenth-century houses along the Green. Here the air was fragrant with the musky scent of trees after rain. He turned down Dawson Street and then into one of the narrower streets that lead towards Grafton Street. A group of teenagers were queuing in a night-club doorway.

He kept on walking, and crossing the Halfpenny Bridge, found himself in a maze of unfamiliar streets leading off the quays. He wasn't sure where he was going or for how long he would continue.

Once, back in Boston, he had spent a whole night walking the city streets. It was the night Jessica had locked him out of the house, the night she had learnt of his affair with Laura Johnson. He had tried sleeping in the car, but after a couple of cramped, sleepless hours in the back seat, he had gone out into the neighbourhood streets.

He had walked for hours that night, through the silent leafy Boston suburbs, and as dawn rose over the city he watched porch lights being switched off and window blinds raised, until gradually he became aware of the low hum of distant traffic as people began leaving for work.

He had gone in somewhere and had a coffee and waited until he was certain that Jessica had gone to work, before making his way back home.

Now as he walked the streets of Dublin, Stuart remembered that night and other, happier, nights with Jessica. He thought too about Laura Johnson and her silken skin, and about a girl in high school called Serena who had taught him how to kiss properly. And about the others he had known — women who had vanished forever from his life, but the memories of whom still lingered, like ghosts, in his mind.

Freak Nights

That summer my mother fell in love with a man who drove an American car. She had been a National School teacher since she was nineteen but she lost her job the previous Christmas because, she said, she didn't believe in God or the educational system any more. So in the spring she packed up, took me out of fourth class and we moved to a small house in the middle of the country that belonged to one of her distant relatives.

From the front window of this house you could see fields and trees and, through the trees, the flat edge of a lake. Sometimes you could see a tractor crossing one of the fields or hear the noises of animals being driven along the road.

At heart my mother was a social person. She liked getting dressed up and going out and meeting people and it must have seemed strange to her to have ended up in this out-of-the-way place, waiting for some kind of news from the world again.

But one evening a man turned up at the back door holding a battered oil can. He said he had an overheated car down the road and needed water for the radiator.

"Oh well," my mother said, "you might as well stay for tea now."

The man's name was Barney and he ran a garage on the outskirts of town. He had dark shoulder-length hair and a salt-and-pepper beard and he had the name of some woman (an Argentinian transvestite, my sister Sinéad later claimed) tattooed on each forearm. He didn't look the type of man my mother would have much to do with, but my father had been gone almost two years and I suppose she didn't give it a lot of thought.

Towards the end of May Sinéad came home on her holidays with her records and her boarding-school ways. She was thirteen-and-a-half and somehow my mother managed to keep her in an expensive school. Maybe she felt life was easier without someone like her around. Sinéad said she thought this new place was the absolute sticks and that our mother must be finally off her rocker. She said she would have it all out with her one of these days.

Because of Sinéad my mother never brought Barney into the house any more. But Sinéad would watch from her bedroom window as they drove off together in the evening. Then she would ask me questions. Did I ever see them kissing? Had he ever been in the house late at night? She thought he looked mean and moody. She said our mother could imagine she was a gold-digger but she would soon have to change her tune. She could tell the guy was only in his twenties and our mother was just trying to make herself feel young again. Women of our mother's age were like that, she knew. But Sinéad soon lost interest in all that. She longed for exciting things to happen in her own life, I suppose.

In the old days, when she was a full-time teacher and supporting my father to all intents and purposes, my mother would spend the holidays working in the garden, dishing out jobs to keep Sinéad and myself occupied. Now she would get up around midday and lounge about in her dressing-gown until well into the afternoon. Then she would cook something quick for us and begin to get ready for the evening. She would wash her hair, put on lipstick and do up her eyes. She started wearing short skirts and hot pants with high black boots. Once, she stood in the kitchen with her hands on her hips and asked us how we thought she looked. "You look just like a tart, I think," Sinéad said. She stared at Sinéad for a few seconds and said in a quiet voice, "Don't ever use that word around here again." She went upstairs then and didn't come down for an hour. "She's probably bawling her eyes out up there," Sinéad said. "It's so embarrassing, I don't know how you can stand it."

Sinéad kept to herself if she could help it. She did enough cleaning to stop my mother nagging, whenever the humour hit her, but she spent most of the day in the front room watching tennis on BBC television.

When we were left alone she would put on a stack of records, drape herself across the couch and light long French cigarettes. I would hang around in the smoky room until I got tired listening to her complaining about life with our mother in this God-forsaken dump.

Then one day Sinéad had a friend—a tall girl with thin legs and flat fair hair called Dolores who had a summer job in Smith's grocery and bar.

At the start Dolores would stand in the kitchen doorway, watching Sinéad eating toast and marmalade. "Don't you ever worry about your complexion?" she would ask.

"What's the point in worrying," Sinéad would reply and Dolores would spend a few minutes carefully examining her finger-nails. Dolores would say, standing there, "My hair will never look as long as yours, never in a million years." Then

Sinéad would pull her hair forward and shake it out and nibble a few ends and say nothing.

Most of the time Dolores would talk about things in her school—a teacher or another girl. Sinéad would look at her, drag on her cigarette and make lazy smoke rings that rose and disappeared just below the ceiling. When Dolores had finished Sinéad would smile, at no one in particular, and say, "You don't have to tell me that, you know." Or she would just start humming to herself while she turned the radio tuner searching for some pirate music station.

After a while Sinéad would get up and pour herself a glass of water. "I'm so bored," she would say. Then Dolores would look as if she was trying hard to think of something interesting to say next.

When she wasn't talking Dolores' gaze would wander around the kitchen. If she spotted something new to her she would stare at it. The first time she saw Sinéad making toast she said, "Oh, you've got a real toaster." For days afterwards, depending on her mood, Sinéad would come into the kitchen and pick up a spoon or my bowl of corn flakes or whatever and waltz around singing, "Oh, you've got a real spoon" or "Oh, you've got a real cup." "Oh, you've got a real brain." She called Dolores Mary Hick and Dopey Doles behind her back, but most of the time she seemed glad to have her around.

I suppose it was because she was bored that Sinéad thought up freak nights. She told Dolores to bring anything she could find. "The more disgusting the better."

Next evening Dolores arrived with a pair of shiny curtains and a bag of old clothes. They spent a few evenings cutting and sewing. In the end they had multi-coloured velvet shirts, long loose dresses and slinky silk jackets—what Sinéad called "kimonos."

Early the following evening Sinéad closed the curtains in the front room. She lit a stick of incense and put it in a glass in the middle of the floor. Then the two of them sat on cushions by the bookcase, in their bright and strange clothes, smoking and listening to loud music.

For the second or third freak night Dolores brought two bottles of Babycham. She was grinning as she took them from her shoulder bag and put them on the kitchen table. Sinéad examined the foil around the neck of each bottle.

"Did you buy these?" she said.

"Mr Smith said I could take them."

"Oh really?" Sinéad said. "Free, gratis and for nothing, I suppose."

"Yes," Dolores said.

Sinéad began to peel away the foil.

"You can't fool us, but we won't say a single word," she said, smiling.

Later, Sinéad said, "You probably don't know this, but vodka is the coolest. No one can ever smell that off your breath."

The next evening Dolores brought a naggin of Smirnoff.

"Oh God," Sinéad said, "oh golly God."

What did I do? Sometimes I was allowed to play the records. I would put on an old pair of my mother's sunglasses and Sinéad would make me wait while she teased and brushed my hair until it stood out in a frizzy bush. Then I would sit back to front on a chair by the record player and put on the songs they called out.

Sinéad and Dolores would get up and dance and call each other "babe" and "love child." They would shout "right on" and "cool" and "far out." Every so often one or the other would start laughing and have to sit down for a few minutes. For some songs I would flick the light off and on until one night Sinéad made me stop because, she said, she didn't want a dead body on her hands.

During those weeks my mother never came home until after midnight, but Sinéad always made sure we had everything cleared up well before then. Dolores said we were lucky. If it was her house her father would beat her black and blue. "Parents aren't a problem if you know how to handle them," Sinéad told her.

Late at night, as I lay in bed listening to the American car idling on the roadside, hearing the low voices, and waiting for the lights to sweep across the ceiling, I wondered if our lives had changed forever.

One evening Dolores gave everyone a fright. She was out dancing on her own, waving her arms and shaking her body in an unusual way. Next thing she was sitting on the floor, holding her head and moaning. Sinéad got down on her knees beside her. "Turn off that fucking music," she shouted.

Dolores' face was pale and wet and her eyes were shut. I started to laugh for some reason.

"Shut up," Sinéad screamed.

She shook Dolores and slapped her face. Dolores put a hand to her cheek and turned her head to one side. Sinéad crouched closer.

"It's nothing, isn't it, Dolores? Tell me it's really nothing at all," she whispered.

She slapped Dolores' face again.

"Say something, you bitch."

After a few seconds Dolores said, "No, it's nothing."

Her face was white. Her eyes were open, but they were staring out beyond us.

Midsummer's Day. Sunlight lay creased across the floor and walls of the front room. Someone was walking around the house, looking in the windows and knocking on the doors. We sat beneath the window, listening. Sinéad held the bottle tightly in her arms.

"It's a man," she said.

"I bet it's the parish priest," Dolores said. "He wants to speak to your mother."

Sinéad started to giggle.

Sinéad lit a cigarette. She was wearing a pair of glasses with blue plastic frames and deep orange lenses. She was looking at Dolores and myself, laughing.

"Everybody has to try this," she said and she reached across and stuck a pair on me.

The room turned red and filled with shadows. We were all grinning. Then we sat there, watching each other.

"This is great," Sinéad said. "We could be in San Francisco, in a park somewhere."

She was right. At that moment we looked like people in another place.

One hot night Sinéad decided to move everything out to the back garden. She put the record player on the window ledge, turned the volume up all the way and wandered around beating down the nettles and the ox-eye daisies with a floor brush. Dolores stood by the back door biting her nails. She said, "What if somebody hears the music?" but Sinéad gave her one of her looks.

I was making toast when I saw that someone had left the vodka on the kitchen table. I poured half of it into a Coke bottle and brought it up to the box-room.

I swallowed a mouthful. My eyes filled with water. I sat on the floor and took another drink. Then I lay back and waited for whatever was supposed to happen. I examined the cracks in the ceiling to see if they would change. I heard the thump of the music from the garden. Sinéad called my name from somewhere. "The little bastard," I heard her say.

I thought I should test my memory. I tried to remember my father, his features and expressions, but they kept on fading and I ended up listing out the things he had left behind. "Useless things," my mother called them. And, I suppose, they would seem so to most people. For example: a guitar with a warped neck, a set of books called *The History of Mathematics*, a bag of wooden golf clubs, a shotgun, its barrel blocked with aircraft modelling cement. When we moved from the city all this stuff was dumped, but I took the shotgun with me and hid it behind a press in my room. I had some idea of using it for hunting.

I thought of a field somewhere with a flock of white birds rising into the air and my father standing in the middle, an arm raised towards the sky, shouting something I couldn't hear because of the beating of the wings.

It was dark when I heard the car pulling up outside. The house was quiet, but the music was still on in the garden. I remember getting the gun from my room and going down the stairs.

Outside, the warm air washed across my face and along my arms. A match flared in the distance. I took a few steps and the night lit up and filled with sounds. People seemed to be moving around on the edge of the darkness. Somebody was speaking in a low steady voice. Someone was crying or laughing. I stared into the light. I opened my mouth and waited for the words to make sense.

Then I felt a hand gripping my shoulder. A man's voice said, "It's all right. The kid's just juiced to the gills, that's all."

My mother never talked about what happened that night, but it was the last time she met Barney.

A few nights later he parked in front of the house and sat in the car, blowing the horn. My mother watched from the darkened landing until he got tired and drove away.

Another night he switched off the engine and sat on the bonnet. I could see the glow as each cigarette he lit hovered in the darkness. "He has no sense," I heard my mother say to herself, but it seemed to me that sense had nothing to do with it.

Dolores disappeared from our lives too, though sometimes one of us would catch sight of her as she hurried to or from the village in a pale blue housecoat.

A small fat woman, wearing black canvas shoes, called to the house one afternoon and spent a short time with my mother in the front room. Afterwards, Sinéad said this was Dolores' mother. She said Dolores' mother had said that she had had high hopes that Dolores would become a nun one day, but that we had put the kibosh on that. "What a laugh," Sinéad said.

Sinéad said our mother was too soft and she shouldn't even consider talking to that awful woman. "I wouldn't have much pity for silly little girls who steal."

The July weather grew cold and unsettled. Sinéad became more sullen and talked for a while about running away from home. My mother stayed in all day, drinking tea and watching television. Sinéad said that she was in emotional trauma and that she was probably planning to change her ways so that she wouldn't bring calamity on her family again.

Perhaps our parents' world always seems less complicated than it really is. But generally people get on with things and within a year we had moved again. Sinéad started day school in a new town. My mother put an ad in the local paper and opened a playschool.

Dolores became a teacher or a bank clerk and ended up living in the city.

Barney would have stayed, though. His car, the wonder of our age, would have skidded and crashed during an icy spell a couple of winters later. After a few half-hearted attempts to make it roadworthy again he would have pushed it into the yard by the side of the garage and watched it turn to rust.

He is happy with his life, though he wonders sometimes about marrying and bringing up children. He considers selling out and going into the video-rental business or emigrating to Australia or the States. But he does none of these things.

He doesn't think very often about my mother or their glory days. Except sometimes, when he gets a bit drunk, a certain memory lights up in his mind. A hot evening towards the end of June. The last of the sunlight glints on the faraway lake. A powder-blue Pontiac is parked outside Smith's grocery and bar. A woman is standing by the open door on the passenger side, running her fingers through her long damp hair. Suddenly she leans forward to check herself in the wing mirror.

Barney remembers this though he's not sure why. It could be from some film he's seen on TV. The heat of the evening, the distant water, the woman by the car, expecting the man who might save her life to appear at any moment.